"Don't take this personally,"

Hallie said, trying to loosen Quade's hold on her on the dance floor, "but you're drooling in my ear."

Quade closed his teeth lightly on her lobe.

Hallie caught her breath, first because Quade was swirling his tongue around the stud in her ear, and second, because she'd seen the guy Quade had pointed out following her.

"Don't eat the earrings. They're real." Hallie wrestled out of Quade's grasp.

"Loosen up." Quade closed his arm around her like a vise and pinned her against him. "The idea here is to look like we've got the hots for each other. You've seen that guy before."

"No," she lied.

"So the gasp you made was ecstasy, not recognition."

"You said it yourself—you're irresistible."

Quade's eyes flashed heat. "I should have thrown the pillowcase over your head and returned you to the admiral kicking and screaming."

"Never too late to try."

"Don't tempt me, tough girl. Don't tempt me."

Dear Reader,

Temptation is Harlequin's boldest, most sensuous romance series . . . a series for the 1990s! Fast-paced, humorous, adventurous, these stories are about men and women falling in love—and making the ultimate commitment.

Nineteen ninety-two marked the debut of Rebels & Rogues, our yearlong salute to the Temptation hero. In these twelve exciting books—one a month—by popular authors, including Jayne Ann Krentz, JoAnn Ross and Ruth Jean Dale, you'll meet men like Josh— who swore *never* to play the hero. Dash—who'd protect the woman he loved . . . at any cost. And Trey—he lived life on the edge . . . and wasn't about to be tamed by a beautiful woman.

Twelve rebels and rogues—men who are rough around the edges, but incredibly sexy. Men full of charm, yet ready to fight for the love of a very special woman. . . .

I hope you enjoy Rebels & Rogues, plus all the other terrific Temptation novels coming in 1992!

Warm regards,

Birgit Davis-Todd
Senior Editor

P.S. We love to hear from our readers!

The Patriot
LYNN MICHAELS

Harlequin Books

TORONTO • NEW YORK • LONDON
AMSTERDAM • PARIS • SYDNEY • HAMBURG
STOCKHOLM • ATHENS • TOKYO • MILAN
MADRID • WARSAW • BUDAPEST • AUCKLAND

For Mike, my hero

Published August 1992

ISBN 0-373-25505-5

THE PATRIOT

Prologue

NEVIN MAXWELL LOOKED just the way you'd expect an ex-government intelligence agent to look, which is exactly why no one ever took him for one. Sinfully handsome, suspicious by nature as well as experience, he never took the same route from his house on Long Island to his office in Manhattan twice in the same month.

He'd learned long ago that the best way to hide was in plain sight. His fourth-floor suite was listed as Maxwell and Associates, Private Consultations, on the building directory in the lobby. In the outer room sat a reception desk no one ever used. The telephones never rang. The computer in his private office was rarely turned on. Lining the walls of the inner sanctum were four antique oak cabinets—cabinets that were elegantly crafted, scrupulously polished, and as empty as the ex-agent's heart.

The files were there for appearance—another lesson Maxwell had learned early on in the game. Though usually deceptive, appearance was important. Sometimes vital.

His memory was photographic. Once he'd opened the mail and reviewed any new cases, it was easy to pick up the phone and dial whomever he needed to do the job. He collected the mail every morning from the lockbox in the basement. He never read it in the elevator, didn't so much as flip through it until he was seated at his desk.

It was Maxwell's only steadfast rule. And on the Monday morning when the envelope arrived from Middleburg, Virginia, with a return address he hadn't seen in six years and had prayed to God he'd never see again, he was damn glad to be sitting down. There was no stamp and no postmark. Somehow—and Maxwell knew precisely how—it had found its way into a locked mailbox to which only he and the carrier on this route had keys.

He tore open the flap, withdrew a single, trifolded ivory sheet and read three words scrawled across the middle in black ink: "Urgent. Call me." Then he picked up the phone and dialed a number he sometimes still murmured in his sleep.

1

WHEN THE PHONE RANG at a little past ten on that same Monday morning, Ellison Quade knew it was Maxwell. He wasn't psychic, but he was a cynic, and since the luggage and Reba were waiting for him in the car—her itsy-bitsy teensy-weensy bikini folded inside her wallet, and their flight to Aruba due to leave Dulles in seventy-two minutes—it figured that the caller had to be Maxwell.

Swearing under his breath, Quade walked back to the telephone, picked up the receiver and asked, "Call to wish me bon voyage?"

"Sure thing," replied Maxwell. "Unfortunately, your destination has changed."

"Dammit, Max. Reba's gonna kill me."

"You can sweet-talk her, but don't take all day doing it. You're expected in Middleburg at twelve forty-five. I just talked to the old man. He's holding lunch for you."

Quade knew only one old man in Middleburg, Virginia. Knew him and had good reason to hate him. "Is this a joke?"

"No joke. He asked for you. His granddaughter has run away."

"Smart kid." Quade made a rueful noise, shook a cigarette out of his pack and lit it. "Why me?"

"He wants the best."

"The best'll cost him."

"I told him I thought it might."

"Bump lunch to one-thirty. It'll take me at least half an hour to talk Reba into letting me live."

"I'll tell him," Maxwell said and hung up.

It took Quade forty-five minutes and he had to do a lot more than talk. He made up the time on the freeway, and at one twenty-three stopped his vintage Mustang ragtop outside a pair of tall, black iron gates. Sleet skittered across the silver hood and stuck in his dark eyelashes as Quade rolled down the window and waited for the electric eye on top of the brick wall to trigger the intercom on the gatepost. It took about ten seconds.

"Step out of the car, please."

He knew the drill and did as instructed, unfolding his wallet to show his ID to the camera. The lens clicked, whirred, then zoomed in on the interior of the Mustang. Quade pocketed his wallet and stepped out of the way.

While the camera did its job, he stuffed his hands into the pockets of his gray suede sports jacket and squinted through the icy mist. The house—a Georgian sprawl of wet red brick—was barely visible. He was, Quade thought, one of the few people who understood what could make a person run away from a place like this. The camera stopped taking pictures and the gates swung inward.

"Please drive through, Mr. Quade," said the voice on the other end of the intercom. "The Admiral is waiting for you in the library."

Impatiently, as it turned out, pacing in front of the fireplace. A small forest fire blazed behind the iron-mesh screen, enveloping Hiram Whitcomb, U.S.N., retired, in a hellish glow. Fitting, Quade thought. As he unwound his red muffler, the man he'd last seen at his court-martial six years earlier turned sharply to face him.

"I wasn't sure you'd come."

"And miss an opportunity to watch you squirm and beg for my help? Not a chance."

Quade draped his scarf over the back of the green leather armchair in front of the Admiral's desk. He couldn't quite remember that fresh-faced kid from Annapolis he'd once been, that newly commissioned lieutenant who'd used to drop so eagerly into this chair. So eagerly and so stupidly.

He'd half expected the old man to be in uniform. Instead, the Admiral wore a tweed jacket and trousers, with a white shirt and a gold suede vest. Old Iron Butt, they'd called him. Did he still clank when he sat down?

"You haven't changed," the Admiral said quietly. Quade couldn't decide whether the old man was relieved or disappointed.

"Oh, I've changed," Quade replied evenly. "I'm older, tougher, and a hell of a lot smarter."

"You were always smart." The Admiral briskly crossed the room and sat down at his desk, a Federalist masterpiece crafted of solid cherry. He didn't clank, but sat straight as a mainmast, his palms flat on the polished surface. "Except, perhaps, when it came to women."

"Look who's talking." Quade sat down in the green leather chair and took out his cigarettes. "You mind if I smoke, I hope."

The Admiral pushed a lead-crystal ashtray toward him. "Those things'll kill you."

"So will hard time in Leavenworth." Quade pulled a cigarette out of his pack, snapped open his lighter and bent his head to the flame.

"Only eighteen months. Just enough to season you."

Quade snapped his lighter shut and blew smoke in Hiram Whitcomb's face. "Up yours, Admiral."

"Maxwell said this would cost me. How much?"

"A full pardon and an honorable discharge."

"Impossible."

Quade shrugged. "Difficult, maybe."

"If I couldn't clear you while I was chief of Naval Intelligence, what makes you think I can now?"

"Because now you have a reason to, Admiral." Quade took another drag of his cigarette and smiled. "I'm looking forward to meeting your granddaughter."

"Your father's of the old school," the Admiral reminded him. "A pardon won't mean a tinker's damn."

"He's a hard ass, you mean. Just like you."

"Your father and I were at Annapolis together. I did everything I could for you."

"Everything but spend eighteen months in Leavenworth. Everything but tell Washington *you* left the embassy satchel in Mai Lu's room."

That made the Admiral squirm. "No one held a gun to your head. As I recall, you volunteered."

"As I recall, you talked me into it. Didn't take much, since I already thought you walked on water. Washington'll understand, you said. Healthy young fella after six months at sea. They might give me a wink and slap my hand, you said, maybe confine me to quarters. Next thing I knew, I was being court-martialed."

The Admiral raised his hands and pressed them together, leaving damp palmprints on the desktop. "My granddaughter is very important to me."

He did not, Quade noted, say he loved her. "Are you sure she ran? She wasn't snatched?"

"I'm sure." The Admiral opened his middle desk drawer, took out a postcard and handed it to Quade.

There was a picture of the Griffith Park Observatory on one side, on the other a ten-day-old postmark and a half-dozen terse lines: "I have a job and my own place.

If you send anyone else to bring me back, I'll run so far you'll never find me. Just leave me alone and let me live like a normal person. That's all I want."

"What a close and loving relationship." Quade tossed the postcard on the desk. "How old is she?"

"Twenty-three."

"How you gonna keep her down on the farm, Admiral, if she doesn't want to stay?"

His eyes slipped away from Quade's gaze. "I'm working on that."

"Uh-huh. And why is she so important to you?"

"She's all I have left." The Admiral looked squarely at Quade. "And she's in danger."

"Aren't we all. It's a scary world."

"I hired two private detectives to find her and keep tabs on her. I was inclined to let her have her fling and get it out of her system. The first detective disappeared his third day in Los Angeles. The second one turned up yesterday in Cedars-Sinai with a fractured skull."

The Admiral delved into his desk drawer again and handed Quade a color Polaroid of a laughing, brown-eyed blonde. She had a small nose, not much of a chin, an overlarge mouth and her grandfather's Mount Rushmore jaw. "Looks like you, poor kid. What's her name?"

"Hallie Stockton. She's been gone three weeks."

"Since she's your granddaughter, I trust she knows how to and is capable of fracturing a man's skull."

"She is."

"But you don't think she did."

"Doubtful."

Quade put his cigarette out and the picture back on the desk. "Then why don't you go after her yourself? Give whoever it is who's using her to lure you out of your little fortress here a clear shot at you."

"If I did," the Admiral replied with a stony smile, "you wouldn't get your pardon."

"And my honorable discharge. Don't forget that." Quade put his cigarettes back in his pocket and stood. "If she doesn't come willingly I'll have to grab her. That's kidnapping and a federal rap. Higher risk for me, higher price tag for you if I get caught."

The Admiral's color deepened. "What else do you want? Eighteen months of your life back?"

"If I get nailed, I want you to go to my father and tell him the truth."

"It won't make any difference."

"Not with him, but he might let me see my mother."

"Very well." The Admiral nodded, but again his glance shifted.

"Just in case," Quade added, picking up his muffler and looping it around his neck, "I'll ask Max to remind you."

The Admiral's gaze swung back and locked with Quade's. "That won't be necessary."

"You'd better hope so. You'd also better hope that if you're setting me up like you did in the Philippines, Max never finds out."

"Why in hell would I do that?"

"'Cause you're a scared old man, Hiram. I've been living in your backyard for three years now. That's bound to make you nervous. Maybe somebody's after you and maybe not. If they are, maybe you'll get lucky and they'll kill me. Or maybe you sent those two P.I.'s out there to make sure you get lucky."

"If I wanted you dead," the Admiral replied tersely, "I wouldn't have to send you to California to see it done."

"Good point."

"I take it this means you won't be staying for lunch."

"I'll pass, thanks."

"When will you leave for Los Angeles?"

"As soon as an envelope from the Department of the Navy shows up in my mailbox."

"I'll expect daily reports."

"You'll get them."

"Why did you come back to Washington?"

"Just to tick off my father. I see him from time to time, you know. He walks past me like I'm not even there."

He didn't tell the Admiral the truth. That he'd come back to see his mother, that he'd used to haunt Bethesda when he wasn't on a job for Max in hopes of catching her alone, that he'd managed it once outside her hairdresser's. She'd blinked in surprise, turned her head away and said, "I can't see you. Not like this." Then she'd climbed into her car and driven away without a backward glance.

Since then, he'd had a recurring nightmare. He dreamed he saw her again on the street and chased her for blocks, screaming her name while she walked faster and faster and he ran slower and slower. He didn't tell the Admiral that he always woke up from that nightmare with tears on his face.

Instead, he said, "If I don't find your granddaughter in L.A. or a detective in Cedars-Sinai with a fractured skull, I'm gonna come back here and make you one *sorry*, scared old man."

He walked out of the house into an ice storm. That evening he repacked his suitcase. His sports gear came out, his working gear went in—gear that was mostly plastic, tucked into places where the X-ray machines at Dulles would never detect them.

On Wednesday the Department of the Navy envelope arrived. Inside were honorable-discharge papers duly sealed and assigned to Lieutenant Ellison Quade III with a note from the Admiral: "The pardon will arrive when my granddaughter is safely home."

Late that night, Quade boarded the red-eye for Los Angeles.

2

A LIFETIME OF LIVING with the Admiral had given Hallie sonar as sensitive as any of the navy's high-tech equipment. Still, he managed to find a table—no easy feat in The Covey's "Thursday Nite Is Ladies Nite" crowd, order a drink—Scotch and water, no ice—and down about a third of it before her internal scope bleeped.

Not a good sign. It meant the Admiral had sent in a big gun a lot sooner than she'd expected. Had her postcard really teed him off? Or was he still working that tired old you're-in-danger-come-home-at-once ploy? Probably both, she decided, as she picked up a tray full of drinks.

While she waited on her customers, Hallie kept an eye on the guy in the gray silk Italian suit. He stayed about an hour, had one drink, smoked two cigarettes and left. All the way home, she looked for a tail that never materialized.

Friday morning she went shopping, lay on the beach behind her rented house and read for a while. In the afternoon she went to a Tupperware party thrown by one of the waitresses at The Covey. Hallie had never been to one before, had an absolute ball, and spent $237.12.

There was no tail, no shadow, but he was at the club again that night, sitting at one of Gwen's tables, flirting with her, pumping her. He never once glanced in Hallie's direction. *Smart cookie.*

When Gwen took a break she asked Hallie to cover for her and be extra nice to the gorgeous guy at table six. The

Employees Only door had no sooner swung shut behind
Gwen when he signaled to Hallie and pointed at his
empty glass. She nodded, went to the bar for a Scotch
and water, no ice, and walked it to his table.

He sat with his chair facing the bandstand, turning one
of The Covey's gold-on-black matchbooks end over end
on the table edge in time to the rock music screaming out
of the man-size speakers. Good sense of rhythm, great
hand-eye coordination. *Nice gray eyes,* Hallie thought,
as she put his drink down in front of him and he nodded. *Nice but cold.*

"Tell my grandfather," she said, leaning forward on her
hands so he could hear her, "to go fornicate with the farm
animals."

Then she went back to the bar to talk to Jesus. He
planned to visit a distant cousin in Rio de Janeiro, so she
was teaching him Portuguese in her spare time. When she
next glanced at table six, the gorgeous guy with the cold
gray eyes was gone. Gwen was not a happy camper.

Neither was Hallie when she got home, turned on her
bedside lamp and saw The Covey matchbook lying on
her pillow. The security system was on—it had beeped
when she'd let herself in—but she raced to the walk-in
closet in the living room to check it, anyway. It was still
on. *Damn* smart cookie. Hallie doubled her fist on the
wall beside the control panel and leaned her forehead
against it. She was shaking.

"Tough guy, huh?" the smart cookie said from behind
her.

"Tough *girl.*" Hallie snapped her head around and saw
him standing in the closet doorway. "It's hard to tell, I
know, but take my word for it."

"Not that hard," he replied, leaning one shoulder against the doorframe. "Your system isn't worth beans. Take my word for it."

"It's top-of-the-line, state-of-the-art."

He folded his arms and smiled at her with all the warmth of a glacier. "So am I."

"Is this where you throw a pillowcase over my head and lock me in the trunk of your car?"

"No." He straightened away from the doorframe. "This is where we talk about how to avoid that."

Then he backed out of the doorway and stepped to one side, clearly waiting for her to precede him. Like the gentleman he appeared to be, may in fact have been at some point in his life, but the gentleman Hallie knew damn well he wasn't. Appearances, she'd learned early on, were always deceptive.

But sometimes an appearance was all you had, so she walked past him like her insides weren't jumping the way they had when the two-point tremor had shivered through the Los Angeles basin the week before. He followed her down the three steps from the entry level into the living room, across the plush dusty-rose carpet to a pale gray sectional in front of the stone fireplace.

The couch came with the lease on the house. The marina-blue throw cushion Hallie picked up and tucked in her lap as she plunked herself down in the curve of the sofa was hers. She'd bought it at The May Company, had spent a whole afternoon her first week in L.A. splitting it open, wedging an old and rusty but very thick and very heavy cast-iron griddle inside and sewing it up again.

He stopped a couple of feet shy of the sofa and gave the house the once-over. It was all glass and white textured walls, vaulted ceilings and polished teak. No doubt he'd already gone over every inch of it with a fine-tooth comb, but he managed to look convincing.

"You call this living like a normal person?" he asked.

"Reading other people's mail is a crime, you know."

"So's kidnapping," he said, taking his cigarettes out of his inside coat pocket. His cigarettes and two airline tickets in folded paper jackets. One-way from LAX to Dulles, Hallie was certain. He tossed them on the glass table in front of the sofa and lit up as he sat down. "Your choice."

"Ho-ho-ho and a bottle of rum."

"So where d'you keep the pillowcases?"

"Oh spare me."

"Exactly what I'm trying to do, tough girl."

He wore another Italian suit, an icy shade of deep-sea blue. The expertly tailored silk made his eyes look the same color and about the same temperature as the Pacific at twenty thousand feet.

"My name's Hallie. What's yours?"

"Quade."

"Something Quade or Quade something?"

"Something Quade."

"So what do I call you?"

"Quade."

"Tough guy, huh?"

He didn't reply, just lifted his right hand to take another drag of his cigarette. On his left wrist he wore a gold watch with a black face. Thin, obviously expensive.

"I'm not going back," Hallie told him.

"Yes you are. It's merely a question of how." Quade put out his cigarette in a pink marble ashtray and stood. "Pillowcase or plane ticket. Pick one."

"Eat rocks," Hallie retorted, lifting her chin to look at him. "Big sharp ones."

"Give it up, tough girl. You ain't got a chance."

"Says you."

"Say your farewells and give your notice. I'll be here tomorrow night to help you pack. The plane leaves at nine forty-five Sunday morning."

"Have a nice trip." Hallie gave him a toothy smile and tightened her grip on the marina-blue pillow.

Quade took a step closer to loom over her, a familiar tactic frequently used by the Admiral. It had long ago ceased to intimidate her. "You're going with me," he said. "One way or the other."

"Says you," Hallie repeated, lifting her chin another fraction to lock her gaze with his. Dumb move, she realized half a second later, when Quade seized the moment's distraction to snatch the cushion from her and toss it Frisbee-style across the room.

With his left hand, no less, Hallie thought dismally, as both she and Quade watched it sail across the room. Handsome as the devil and ambidextrous, too. The cushion slammed into and exploded a crystal lamp atop a teak credenza, raining diamond shards of leaded glass all over the carpet.

"Cute trick," Quade said, looking back at her. "Is that what you used to bash in the side of Ferguson's head?"

"Which one's Ferguson? The tall one or the dumpy one?"

"The tall one. He's in ICU at Cedars-Sinai with a fractured skull. The dumpy one is a P.I. out of D.C. named Kazmerchek. Nobody's seen him since he left The Covey at closing time two weeks ago yesterday."

"Give it up, Quade." Hallie got to her feet and thrust her hands on her hips. "I don't scare easy."

"We'll see about that, tough girl." A frigid hint of a smile touched one corner of his mouth, then he turned away from her and walked up the steps into the closet.

Hallie followed and watched Quade punch four digits into the security system's number pad. The right four, she thought sourly, as the little red lights winked off.

"How long did it take you to figure out the code?"

"'Bout twenty seconds."

The system allowed sixty before triggering the alarm. Hallie's heart sank, but she kept her chin up as she backed away and let Quade walk past her to the front door.

"Change the code," he said, looking at her with one hand on the knob. "It won't stop me, but it might somebody else."

He let himself out and shut the door. Hallie followed, slipping outside onto the redwood deck built around the beach house. There was no sign of Quade. She didn't turn on the light, just stood in the warm dark, listening. For the sound of his footsteps, a car engine—anything— but there was only the hiss of the ocean, like a radio turned low and not quite tuned to a station.

"Just what I need, a freaking Ninja," Hallie muttered, then went back inside and slammed the door.

She threw the dead bolt, hooked the chain and launched a search for the bugs she knew Quade had planted. She found three, took the lid off the toilet tank and ceremoniously drowned them one at a time. If he hadn't shaken her confidence so profoundly, if it didn't feel so good to beat him at his own game, it might have dawned on Hallie that finding the bugs had been just a little too easy.

Smiling, she flushed the toilet and went into the closet to change the code. She entered the first four prime numbers that came into her head. One single digit and three double. It might slow Quade up for an additional ten seconds, Hallie thought, and felt her smile fade.

If she was lucky.

3

THE ADMIRAL SAID THERE was no such thing as luck, only opportunity. The trick was being sharp enough to recognize it, quick enough to grab it and ruthless enough to use it. It was the only thing her grandfather ever said that Hallie agreed with.

All day Saturday she spent envisioning opportunities and planning how best to make use of them. Thinking ruthless gave her trouble until she reminded herself what life was like in Middleburg and how much worse it would be if she let Quade drag her back. After that, merciless was no problem.

Just in case he was watching—and she could almost feel his cold gray eyes riveted between her shoulder blades—Hallie packed her suitcases, drove into L.A. and closed her bank account. A fistful of American Express traveler's checks went into her purse; a money order for three months' rent and an extra five hundred to cover the crystal lamp went into an envelope with a note to her landlord.

She dropped it in the mailbox in front of the bank, hitched her leather tote over her shoulder, walked back to her rented silver IROC-Z Camaro, unlocked the door and slid in behind the wheel. She started the engine, put on her sunglasses and adjusted the rearview mirror.

"Figure this out, tough guy," she said to the reflection of her frosted lenses. "Am I going along with you or just making it look like I am?"

It was one or the other, and he couldn't be sure. The uncertainty would make him warier and more dangerous, but it would also keep him off balance. Not much of an edge, but Hallie would take whatever she could get.

On the drive back to Malibu, she stopped at her favorite taco joint. She ordered her usual two bean-and-chile burritos, then walked around the counter under an archway with arrows pointing to the rest rooms. The beach was twenty minutes down the road, and it was, she figured, just about time for the giant-size soda she'd drunk on her way into L.A. to hit her.

There were two pay phones in the hallway, one on the left by the men's, one on the right by the ladies'. Both were invisible from the restaurant. Hallie made her call, nipped into the bathroom to flush the toilet, crank a faucet on and off, then hurried back to the counter, wiping her fingers on her jeans as if they weren't quite dry.

She paid for her take-out with a ten and drove home, put the Camaro in the garage, let herself into the house, shut off the alarm and raced for the bathroom. Then she ate her lunch, took a shower and started getting ready for work.

At five-thirty Hallie set the alarm, put her suitcases in the trunk and climbed behind the wheel in a turquoise suede minidress with fringe and beadwork on the bodice, three more inches of knotted fringe at the hem and over-the-knee boots to match. In her double-pierced ears she wore turquoise-and-sterling-silver wires and quarter-karat diamond studs. If opportunity failed, she'd wear the outfit home on the plane. The Admiral would have a stroke.

At ten-thirty or so, as she hung over the bar listening to Jesus conjugate verbs while he loaded her tray, Hallie's back started to itch between her shoulder blades. Turning her head to the right, she glanced up and saw Quade threading his way toward a staircase, one of five spirals winding down to the dance floor. He wore the gray suit again, the silk shimmering chartreuse in the green neon light from the tubes outlining the banister and the guardrail around the upper level.

The sight of him coming down the stairs made her stomach clench. *Just anxiety,* she told herself, then picked up her tray and went to serve her tables. It took nearly twenty minutes to make her rounds in the Saturday night crush. When she came back with her empties and a new batch of orders, Quade was leaning against the bar, fingers capped over the rim of a Scotch and water, no ice.

He raised his chin as Hallie slid her tray across the bar, turned his head to look her square in the eye and smiled. It wasn't much of a smile, tentative, quirky, but it made him look almost human. Hallie was stunned, watched him pick up his glass, take a drink and put it down again without breaking eye contact. The overhead track lights turned his hair blue, the smile that spread across his face again turned the inside of her mouth to dust.

My God, he's flirting with me, Hallie realized, and felt herself go cold all over. She'd been hit on often enough, usually because she was the Admiral's granddaughter. When Quade tossed off the rest of his drink and started edging toward her through the customers stacked three-deep at the bar, she looked swiftly at Jesus and began reading her orders to him. Her voice and hands were steady, but her fingers felt like thumbs as she finished flipping through her pad, told Jesus in Spanish to get the lead out, and made a quick scan in search of Quade.

Either he'd been out in the sun too long or something was up. Something big to make him behave like Joe Cool out cruising for babes. The one scenario was as scary as the other—scary enough to throw her senses on red alert as she made another sweep of the partying crowd and felt a hand settle lightly on her left elbow.

His fingers were warm, which amazed Hallie almost as much as the fact that Quade had somehow managed to outflank her in this mob. Warily, she glanced at him over her shoulder. The ice she'd expected to feel in his touch was still in his eyes.

"So what d'you think, tough girl?" He kept his voice low, bent his right elbow on the bar and pinched a length of fringe on her bodice between his left thumb and forefinger. "Can you handle those two goons who tailed you all day? Or should I hang around?"

He twisted the tiny suede knot between his fingers and stared at the front of her dress like there was something there worth looking at. Since fraternization was encouraged rather than prohibited by the manager, Hallie didn't slug him. She merely said sweetly, "You're the only goon *I* see."

Quade raised just his eyes to her face and smiled that quirky damn smile again. "Very funny, tough girl." He gave her fringe a suggestive little tug, straightened, slid his right hand down her left arm and closed his thumb and middle finger around her wrist. "Let's dance," he said, and yanked her away from the bar.

Walking briskly with his left hand in his trouser pocket, Quade towed her behind him, his grip as loose as a bangle until she tried to wrench free. Then the finger bracelet tightened like a manacle. All Hallie could do was twist around to wave at Jesus and point to Gwen and her tray.

The sound system was on, the band on break between sets. Too bad, Hallie thought, as Quade dragged her up onto the dance floor during a lull between numbers. It would have been interesting to see what he did with heavy-metal rock.

A ballad with acoustic guitars, a weepy trombone and a Latin rhythm began, "Almost in Love," by Elvis, from his movie *Live a Little, Love a Little. Now there's irony for you,* Hallie thought. A little life of her own was all she'd ever wanted. And if opportunity failed to knock before nine forty-five tomorrow morning, that's all she'd get—a little. Very little. Three and a half weeks' worth.

Twirling her around by the wrist, Quade pulled her tight against him and started moving to the music. À la Kevin Bacon, with his right hand pressed to the small of her back, his left hand still in his pocket. Very smooth, very sexy. Designed to throw her off balance, and it might have worked if he hadn't whispered in her ear, "Don't take this personally, tough girl. It's for the benefit of our audience."

Hallie pried herself off his chest and held him at arm's length. "What audience?"

"Upstairs by the door," Quade answered, guiding her through a deft turn in perfect time to the music.

It took her a minute to locate him, leaning on one foot against the wall with a longneck in his hand. The backwash from a nearby freestanding neon sculpture cast his sharkskin jacket and pleasant but unmemorable features in an eerie Halloween glow. Just another guy on the prowl, except that his gaze, when it slid over the dance floor, lingered on Hallie and Quade for a fraction longer than was casual.

"At the table by the bandstand with the blonde," Quade added, pulling her close to nuzzle the curve of her neck and ease her through another turn.

"Don't take this personally," Hallie said, trying to wriggle free of him again, "but you're drooling in my ear."

"You wish," Quade replied, and closed his teeth lightly on her lobe.

"Had all your shots?"

"Lose the jokes and look, will you?"

Hallie did and caught her breath, first because Quade was swirling his tongue around the stud in her ear, and second because she'd seen the guy before. But not today. She'd felt strongly that someone had been watching her, but she'd been looking for cold gray eyes, warm hands, lean, hard thighs—

"Don't eat the earrings. They're real." Hallie wrestled out of Quade's grasp and drew a quick, steadying breath.

"Loosen up." Quade closed his arm around her like a vise and pinned her against him. "The idea here is to look like we've got the hots for each other."

"Oh, gag me." Hallie made a face and started to stick her finger down her throat.

Quade's hand flashed out of his pocket, caught hers and drew it inside his suit coat. Seductively he rubbed her palm over the pebbled grip of the gun holstered to his rib cage. The piece felt thin and flat, like a sleek semiautomatic, the muscle beneath it like tempered steel.

"I'd just as soon not use that to get us out of here."

"Spare me, tough guy," Hallie retorted. "I told you I don't scare easy and I'm not stupid. Neither one of those characters followed me anywhere today."

"How would you know? You were too busy looking for me."

"What are you, clairvoyant?"

"No. Irresistible. You've seen the guy with the bimbo before, haven't you?"

"No, oh great mystic seer, I haven't."

"So the gasp you made was ecstasy, not recognition."

"You said it yourself—you're irresistible."

"I should've thrown the pillowcase over your head when I had the chance."

"Never too late to try."

"Don't tempt me, tough girl. Don't tempt me."

4

ANYONE ELSE WOULD HAVE strangled her by now, but Quade was his usual frigid, unflappable self. The odds against opportunity were rapidly approaching astronomical. What Hallie needed was a diversion, and the only one she had was the goon gazing at the bimbo and tracing circles on her wrist with a very large thumb.

"Now that you mention it," she said, letting her eyebrows draw thoughtfully together, "there is something kind of familiar about that guy."

"Do tell. How familiar?"

"I could swear I've seen him before, but maybe I've just got him mixed up with Schwarzenegger. He's about Arnold's size, even looks a bit like him, and I did watch *Predator* on cable last night."

"You watched *An Affair to Remember*," Quade told her. "You cried through the last seventeen minutes, blew your nose six times, cussed the Admiral up one side, me down the other, and shut the TV off at three forty-seven."

"Funny." Hallie tilted her head to one side. "You don't look like a Peeping Tom."

"I'm not."

"Don't tell me, tough guy. I drowned your three little bugs in the toilet."

"I planted five."

Oh, hell. Hallie felt herself go cold all over.

"You sleazy son of a—" she began, then bit her tongue as Quade gave her a quick chuck under the chin. Reflex brought tears to her eyes and she tasted blood.

"Watch your mouth." He smiled his quirky, hey-baby smile, but his voice was like sleet. "It's not nice to swear at the guy who's trying to dance you into bed."

"It's not nice to bug my house." Hallie glared at him and willed her miserably throbbing tongue to stop. "It's dirty pool."

"Rule number one. Never play fair. Now wipe that look off your face and remember we've got an audience."

"Guess I should remember who you work for, too." Hallie blinked madly at the tears in her eyes. She hated to cry.

"That's rule number two. Pick a side, any side, and stick to it." He touched his thumb to the corner of her mouth, his voice still sleety. "No matter what."

Elvis and the weepy trombones faded away. Quade lifted his hand from the small of her back, his thumb from her mouth. Nonplused, he glanced at the blood on the pad and rubbed it away on his finger.

"Where have you seen him?"

"I don't remember." Hallie about-faced on one two-inch suede heel. Quade's hand clamped around her right elbow.

"Don't screw with me, tough girl." He locked her hip against his thigh and started weaving a path through the couples starting to dance to the Righteous Brothers. "Where've you seen him?"

"I don't remember," Hallie repeated belligerently.

"C'mon, Rhodes scholar. You can do better than that."

"You're hurting me."

"Not yet I'm not." Quade lifted her off the dance floor, swung her around and backed her against a support column on one of the spiral staircases. He could have slammed her into it hard enough to crush a couple of vertebrae, looked like he wanted to, but didn't.

So much for diversions, Hallie thought, as he let go of her elbow and spread his hands above her shoulders on the backside of one of the risers. "Playtime's over. Ferguson came out of his coma this morning, said to the nurse, 'Oh, my God, it's Conan the Barbarian.' Then he died."

A shiver and the vibration of someone starting down the staircase raced each other up Hallie's spine. The cold wrought-iron burned like dry ice on the back of her neck, but felt about fifty degrees warmer than Quade's eyes looked as he glanced up, then quickly bent his head and buried his lips beneath her upturned jaw.

There was a trill of laughter, the spiky edge of a hand-kerchief hemline skimmed over her hair. Beneath Quade's granite mouth Hallie felt her pulse beat wildly, clenched her teeth and closed her eyes. She opened them when the vibration and the clanking footsteps passed and Quade raised his head.

"Don't lie to me ever again," he said. "You know what I am and what I can do to you if you piss me off one more time. I'm going to kiss you now and you're going to let me. I'll step a little to the right while I'm at it, so you'll be able to see Conan but he won't be able to see you.

"Then we'll walk to the bar. By the time we get there you'll remember where and when you've seen him. If not, I'll let him have you. What's left when he's finished, I'll scrape up in a pillowcase and take home to your grandfather. Understand?"

Hallie nodded. "It's all coming back to me," she said
shakily. She'd known all along where and when she'd
seen Conan, but now she remembered how easy it had
been to get away from Middleburg. And at last she understood why.

Cupping her face in his hands, Quade bent his head
and kissed her. Hallie put her arms around his neck and
let him. She didn't part her lips and neither did he. When
she felt his body shift to the right, she opened her eyes
and looked at Conan. He didn't look at her. His attention was fixed on the bimbo. His circles had climbed up
her arm from the wrist to the inside of her elbow.

Quade broke the kiss, put his arm around her shoulders and walked her back to the bar. Hallie winked at Jesus and held up two fingers. He returned the wink,
delivered a Scotch and water, no ice, and a strawberry
daiquiri, then moved to the far end of the bar and blew
Hallie a kiss.

Quade arched an eyebrow. "You don't drink."

"I don't smoke, either, but I'll have your baby if you'll
give me a cigarette."

He gave her one with a quirky smile, then opened his
lighter and spun the wheel. Hallie put the cigarette between her lips and dipped it into the flame. His hands
were steady, hers were not. The smoke scorched her
throat and burned her eyes, but the rush that came with
her second inhale shot the adrenaline she needed into her
bloodstream. Her insides stopped shaking. In a minute
her fingers would, too.

"I've seen him in D.C. twice in the last four months. I
volunteer at the Smithsonian, but I'm sure you already
know that." Hallie took a third shallow puff on her cigarette. "He was part of my tour for an hour or so one
Wednesday afternoon and then he left. About a week

later—a Monday, I think—he followed me across The Mall. I managed to give him the slip in the Museum of Natural History."

"Did you tell the Admiral?"

"No. I figured the Admiral had hired him. He was into having me followed. Not all the time, just whenever he took it into his head. Spot checks, he called them. He'd hit me with these reports, usually at breakfast so he'd be sure to ruin my day. He'd grill me about where I'd been, who I'd been with. Sometimes he even had snapshots."

"Until you figured out how to play his game." Quade picked up his Scotch and turned around to lean his back against the bar. He raised his glass and drank, let his gaze drift around the room. "You haven't seen Conan since?"

"No." Hallie took a last draw on her cigarette and a sip of her daiquiri. Her hands were steady now. Cautiously she kept the rum away from the raw spot on her tongue and her eyes away from Quade. *Think ruthless*, she told herself. The Admiral can, *he* can, and so, by God, *you* can.

"How did you slip your leash?" Quade slid his hand across her midriff, cupped her right hip and pulled her against him.

"Very carefully. It took me months to set up." Hallie swallowed a mouthful of daiquiri and the bitterness that had come with her realization on the edge of the dance floor. "Four to be exact."

"You think the Admiral let you go." Quade made it a statement, not a question. He did that a lot. It was one of his most arrogant and annoying habits. Ranked right up there with the teasing stroke of his fingers on her hip.

"You bet I do. It was too easy. I thought so then, and I think Conan being here proves it. The question is *why* the Admiral let me go."

It wasn't the only question, but it was the only one Hallie dared voice. If Conan was the Admiral's man, who was Quade? She wouldn't put it past her grandfather to play them against each other, but if Conan was on the same team why had he killed Ferguson? And what had he done with Kazmerchek?

But if he wasn't on the Admiral's side, why had she seen him in Washington? She'd assumed Quade was her grandfather's top gun, but was he? Though he hadn't denied it, he hadn't exactly confirmed it, either. Hallie didn't scare easy, but a man was dead and it looked like the Admiral's you're-in-danger-come-home-at-once ploy wasn't a ploy.

"That does seem to be the question," Quade agreed, raising his Scotch and letting his fingers trail along her rib cage.

His touch made her stomach flutter, her skin *crawl*, Hallie told herself, and tried to make herself believe it as she pushed away from the bar. "We have to leave or I have to go back to work. Gwen won't mind if she thinks you're whisking me off to the nearest motel, but she will if you just stand here panting and pawing."

"I'm not panting, tough girl." He gave her his quirky smile and half turned toward her.

Hallie noticed then that he hadn't lit a cigarette while they'd been standing here. She noticed, too, from the corner of her eye, that Conan's head lifted in their direction as Quade raised his drink to finish it. Quickly, she caught his wrist and leaned up on her toes to kiss his mouth. She couldn't quite stretch that far, so she settled for what she could reach, touching her lips to the curve of his jaw.

Tears sprang in her eyes, from the scrape of his beard against her tongue, she told herself. Hastily Quade put his glass down, gripped her hips and pulled her against him. He made it look convincing, but when Hallie backed away from him she could still see tundra in his gray eyes.

"Get your purse," he said. "Take your car keys out and keep them in your hand."

Hallie nodded and signaled to Jesus. He swung her leather tote over the bar, she took out her keys, closed them in her fist and hitched the bag over her shoulder. Quade steered a course for the closest staircase, stepping aside when they reached it to let Hallie go first.

Halfway up she caught a glimpse of Conan, who didn't so much as flick an eyelash in their direction. Odd, she thought, shifting her gaze to the upper level in search of the guy in the sharkskin jacket. The sculpture he'd been standing next to flashed on and off like a traffic signal. The empty beer bottle resting on the base flickered red, yellow, red—stop, caution, stop.

Too late for either one, Hallie thought, quelling the urge she felt to run up the rest of the steps. Quade came off the spiral behind her, took her elbow and moved her unhurriedly toward the exit.

"Check the empty," she said to him.

"I see it," he replied, pushing them through the door into the glare and blare of Hollywood Boulevard.

The sidewalk was crowded and gritty, the night air thick with exhaust. Quade ducked between two parked cars, caught a break in the traffic and marched Hallie across the street. The lot where she'd parked the Camaro lay between two buildings, small and well lit as a closet.

"Great place for a mugging," Quade said dryly, just as two men got out of a Ford sedan at the back of the lot and started toward them. "What'd I tell you?"

"Only two, tough guy," Hallie replied in a low voice. "Conan must think you're easy."

One of them was the guy in the sharkskin jacket. The other one Hallie never got a good look at, because Quade grabbed her and hurled her away from him with sufficient force to fling her onto a blue Toyota.

The impact left her breathless and sprawled across the hood. Gasping for air, Hallie raised her head, heard a grunt and a thump behind her, and saw her tote bag lying against the windshield. She grabbed it and fumbled it open.

Bone crunched behind her, somebody groaned. Hallie dug her mace canister out of her bag, bit the cap off and spit it out. Pushing up on her elbows, she shifted her keys into her left hand, closed the mace can tightly in her right and twisted around in time to see Quade land a spinning back kick worthy of Chuck Norris on the guy in the sharkskin jacket. He went down in a heap next to his fallen cohort.

"Okay, tough girl?" Quade turned toward her, scarcely breathing hard.

"Yeah, no thanks to you." Hallie peeled herself off the Toyota, stumbled as she wheeled around and fell back against the grill, grabbing her left knee and rolling her shoulder forward to keep the canister hidden. "Ouch! Dammit!"

"Sorry 'bout that." Quade took a step closer and offered his hand.

"So am I, tough guy." Hallie raised the mace, pushed the trigger and gave Quade a faceful.

A fraction too late he swung his head away and fell back staggering. In a flash Hallie was on her feet, her tote flung over her shoulder like a baseball bat. She'd tucked the cast-iron griddle in the bottom that morning she swung it with all her might. The blow caught Quade between his shoulders and spread-eagled him on the Toyota. She hit him again, hard enough to bounce his head on the hood, then ran for her car six parking spaces away.

Her legs shuddered, her back muscles screamed. She was panting and sobbing at the awful thunk Quade's forehead had made, but her hands were steady. She had the door open in seconds, the engine started, her seat belt fastened and the gearshift in reverse. The tires squealed as she backed the car out of its space, shoved the transmission into first and sent the Camaro rocketing past Quade.

In the rearview mirror she stole a quick glimpse of him still facedown on the Toyota, glanced back at the exit and slammed on the brake and the clutch. Over the cars streaking past on Hollywood Boulevard, Hallie saw Conan standing on the sidewalk outside The Covey staring straight at her.

Horror nearly clenched her throat shut. She looked at Quade again in the mirror, saw him writhing and trying to push himself off the Toyota, looked back at Conan and saw him step off the curb. She took her foot off the brake, shifted into reverse and fishtailed the Camaro backward.

In the mirror, Hallie watched Quade shove himself up on one hand and shake his head. She shifted into neutral, stepped on the brake and stretched over the console to pop the door. It flew wide open and would have swept Quade off his feet if he hadn't grabbed the top edge of the window just as Hallie clutched a handful of his left sleeve and yanked him into the car. His head cracked the frame with a sickening thud, but he managed to catch the door and shut it as he fell into the seat.

"Go," he rasped at her, pushing the lock with his elbow and fastening his belt.

Hallie went, shifting gears and praying for the light at the corner to change. It did a second or two before the Camaro hit the exit, hard enough to bottom out. Sparks shot from the undercarriage, the traffic cleared, the digital speedometer read fifty-three miles an hour.

Cutting the wheel hard left, Hallie flipped on the headlights. The beams raked over Conan as he hiked himself onto the back bumper of a parked car and launched himself at the Camaro. He landed on the right rear fender with a whump that nearly snapped the springs, but Hallie changed gears, popped the clutch and hit the gas, and the Camaro shot out from under him. In the rearview mirror she watched him roll off and land on his hands and knees in the middle of Hollywood Boulevard.

"Nice move, tough girl," Quade said raggedly beside her. "No guts, no glory." Then he leaned his head against the side window, closed his eyes and passed out.

Once she'd put a dozen blocks between the Camaro and Hollywood Boulevard, Hallie pressed two fingers to the side of his throat and felt his pulse beating strong and steady. Then she wrapped her left hand around the wheel and her right on the gearshift. Keeping constant watch in her mirrors, she drove as fast as she dared toward Marina del Rey.

She only had to stop once to throw up.

5

THEY WERE AT SEA when Quade came to. Or woke up, he wasn't sure which, but the roll of the ship was the first sensation to permeate the fog clogging his head. At sea and under sail, he realized, recognizing the creak of the timbers, the graceful swoop from wave to trough. God, it felt good. Like the first rush of an orgasm.

He kept his eyes closed and let consciousness return at its own pace. He knew better than to fight or force it, especially since once he was fully awake he knew he was going to hurt like hell. His back was a knotted, twitching mass of muscle spasms; the lump on the left side of his head pulsed every time his heart pumped. By trying to help him, the tough girl had damn near killed him.

Gingerly, he touched his fingers to his skull and winced. Half an inch lower and they'd be sliding him over the side wrapped in a flag. Wondering who "they" might be, Quade opened his eyes and saw the Admiral's granddaughter sitting Indian-style on the opposite bunk watching him.

She wore rolled-up jeans, thick white socks and canvas deck shoes, a navy sweatshirt and an unzipped yellow slicker. She'd scrubbed off her bar-girl makeup, brushed the spritz out of her hair and tied it back at the nape of her neck with a nautical-print scarf. She looked about eighteen, her brown eyes almost amber.

"Hey tough girl." Quade pushed himself woozily up on one elbow, wincing in the blinding sunlight streaming through the ports.

"How d'you feel?"

"Like hell." Quade closed his dry, aching eyes, pressed his thumb and forefinger against his lids, opened them and looked around.

They were in the forward cabin, part galley, part cockpit. By the size of it, he figured aboard a thirty-five-foot schooner. Double mast, two- or three-man crew, at least one more cabin aft. He started to swing his legs over the side, but caught himself when Hallie withdrew his Walther TPH from her lap and leveled it at his chest.

"Does this mean we aren't friends anymore?"

"Rule number three, tough guy," she replied evenly. "Never trust anybody."

"You aren't gonna shoot me." Quade said. "If you'd wanted me dead you would've left me for Conan."

She moistened her bottom lip with the tip of her tongue. "That's what you were going to do to me."

The thought still scared the hell out of her. He could see it in her eyes, in the dilation of her pupils and felt relieved. It was the first sensible reaction he'd seen her exhibit to anything so far.

"I would've if you'd given me any more guff." Quade pushed himself up and sat on the side of the bunk. His left pant-leg was split from thigh to knee, his mouth tasted like bilge.

Hallie raised the Walther an inch and a quarter.

"Give it a rest, will you?" He swallowed thickly and half closed his eyes. The pulse slugging repeatedly against the side of his head eased. Not much, but enough to keep him from retching. He cracked his right eye and saw the bore of the Walther still aimed at his solar plexis. "No hard feelings about last night, tough girl. You did what you had to do. I understand, this is business. I didn't take it personally. Now understand this. If I were stupid enough to leap off this bunk, all I'd be able to do is puke in your lap. In case you've never seen one up close and personal, this is what a concussion looks like."

The Walther didn't waver, but her tongue touched her lip again. "Let's get a couple of things straight first," she said evenly. "One, I'm not going back with you. Two, we're headed for Mexico. When we make port in Ensenada, we'll put you ashore. Three, I keep the gun."

Quade smiled thinly. "Truce terms."

"Take 'em or leave 'em."

"I'll take 'em," he croaked. "Now point me to the head. Quick."

She did with an aftward wave of the Walther. Quade staggered off the bunk and made it just in time. When he came out he felt better. Weaker, but better. Hallie was gone. On the bunk he'd vacated lay a folded pair of weathered jeans, a navy sweatshirt, socks and canvas decks, a red nylon windbreaker and a pair of briefs. He picked them up and checked the size. Thirty-four. He was a thirty-two.

On the ledge beside the bunk sat a steaming white mug, a can of shaving cream, a razor, two squat plastic bottles—one aspirin, the other eye drops—and a pair of wire-frame sunglasses. It was enough to make a strong man cry. Instead he took a shower, shaved himself with a trembling hand, gulped four aspirin with the coffee, squeezed drops into his eyes and got dressed. The jeans were long enough but too big in the waist. He cinched them with his belt. The socks were too tight so he went without, the decks a half size too small but walkable. The sweatshirt gaped at the neck.

There was at least one other man on board his height who had a neck like a bull, weighed between two hundred and two-twenty and liked his beer. Quade put on the shades, found half a loaf of bread and a jar of peanut butter, made a sandwich to save his stomach from the aspirin, chewed it slowly to make sure it would stay down, drank another cup of coffee and wondered who the other guy was.

He could have snooped and found out, but didn't trust himself not to throw up in the chart locker so he skipped it. For now, at least. The roll of the ship didn't faze him, he already had his sea legs. Some things, like riding a bike, you never forgot. Others, like his splitting head, you were a fool to ignore.

"You're eating," Hallie said from the hatchway. She sounded surprised. "I thought you'd still be tossing your cookies."

"Or hoping, maybe?" Quade glanced at her over his left shoulder. He was leaning against the tiny galley sink. She stood on the third step up from the cabin, elbows bent on the hatchway doors. Well-oiled doors, since he hadn't heard her push them open. He'd remember that.

"Maybe." Hallie's eyes gleamed with either mischief or malice. Quade bet on the latter, put his mug down and pushed up his left sleeve.

There was an eagle etched on his forearm, wings spread, beak open, its gaze so fierce it was often mistaken for a buzzard. He didn't think the Admiral's granddaughter would mistake it. She didn't.

"You don't look ex-navy." She pursed her lips and eyed him askance. "Or the tattoo type, either."

"What you get ain't always what you see, tough girl."

"I have a name," she said irritably.

"Who's driving the bus?"

"Arnie Stockton." She smiled, her amber eyes glimmering. "My father."

Quade couldn't have been more surprised if she'd said Fletcher Christian. Her smile arched smugly.

"The Admiral told you he was dead, too, didn't he?"

"No, he never mentioned him. The dossier he keeps on you does, and just to make sure, I checked him out with the Pentagon. He's still listed as MIA."

"He has his reasons." She hesitated a moment, then looked at him squarely, her gaze somber. "The Admiral is one of them."

"How'd you find him?"

"I didn't. He found me." She pivoted on the ball of her foot and looked over her shoulder. "Want to meet him?"

"Why not." Quade zipped his windbreaker and followed her up the hatchway onto the deck.

The glare of the sun on blue water and snowy sail nearly staggered him, but the salty rush of the wind and the crackling canvas overhead restored him. The ship was a honey, a double-masted schooner just as he'd thought, both unfurled sails taut and white. She was racing south off the wind at about six knots, the sun starboard and sinking fast. He'd been out the whole damn day.

"What's her name?" Quade asked, stepping aside to let Hallie shut the cockpit hatch.

"*Halimedes*," she told him, wiping spray off her hands as she straightened beside him, her cheeks flushed, her eyes shining. "My name in Greek. It means thinking of the sea."

Quade said nothing, just followed her toward the stern where Commander Arnold Stockton, U.S.N.—reported missing in action in the Gulf of Tonkin three months before the birth of his only child—stood at the helm of his ship. His reddish-blond beard and hair were sleeked to his head, accentuating the strong bones of his face and skull.

He grinned happily at the sight of his daughter, raised his right hand from the wheel and wrapped his arm around her as she slipped up beside him and laid her hand on his chest. He kissed the top of her head and looked at Quade, no longer grinning, his gaze steady but unreadable.

"This is Something Quade," Hallie told him.

"Arnie Stockton." The Commander uncupped his daughter's shoulder and held out his hand.

Standing at attention, Quade offered his best Annapolis salute. It was rusty but impressive. "Permission to come aboard, Captain."

The Commander's eyebrows shot up, but he returned the salute. Crisply. "Permission granted."

"Nuts," Hallie said and snapped her fingers.

Arnie Stockton threw back his head and laughed. "Is that why you lugged him aboard last night? So I could deny permission to board and you could feed him to the sharks?"

"It occurred to me," Hallie admitted, letting her gaze slide sideways toward Quade.

Her eyes were gleaming again, with triumph rather than malice. Nah-nah-nah-nah, tough guy. She laid her cheek on the Commander's shoulder and gave Quade an I'm-with-my-Daddy-now-and-you-can't-touch-me smile. It was pathetic.

And heartrending.

The wind was beginning to fall, the sails to billow. Off the starboard bow the Pacific shone like quicksilver. Unless Arnie Stockton planned to run all night under power, he'd bring *Halimedes* shoreward soon. Even as

Quade thought it, the Commander was squinting portside where the wafer-thin smudge on the horizon marked the coastline.

"Time to find a safe berth for the night, Mr. Stockton," he said, giving Hallie a smack on the fanny.

"Aye, aye, Cap'n." She gave him a saucy salute and scampered away to man the winch, her face glowing.

"Hallie told me what happened last night," the Commander said to Quade. "I wouldn't mind hearing your version, Mr. Quade, so long as you understand there are other guns besides yours on board and I won't hesitate to use them if necessary."

"It won't be," he replied. "I'll give you until Ensenada. It isn't Something Quade, it's Ellison. I prefer Quade."

The Commander nodded. "Fair enough."

"I'd love to help take her in."

"Tomorrow. You look pretty green around the gills."

"Fair enough. I know my way around the galley."

"Great." Arnie Stockton grinned. "My daughter tells me she can't make toast and I'm afraid I'm not much better."

Quade looked at his watch. "Twenty-hundred okay?"

"It'll do."

It just about would, Quade figured, starting for the hatchway. Hallie ignored him when he passed the winch, but he could feel her amber eyes on his back—even in the cockpit, where he paused to spread his hands on the navigation table and scan the chart tacked to its edges. Bringing *Halimedes* in, finding a safe harbor and making her fast for the night would keep Hallie occupied. He had plenty of time to throw together a meal and comb every inch of the schooner's interior.

Once he'd memorized the course the Commander had plotted for Ensenada, Quade made his way to the aft cabin. He found the arsenal first, picked the lock, opened it and whistled. The contents suggested that Commander Stockton expected trouble from more than the likes of Ellison Quade.

He relocked it and went through the rest of the cabin. By the time he finished he knew why Arnie no longer had a neck like a bull. He also had a fair idea of where he'd spent the past twenty-four years, how he'd managed to contact his daughter, and no doubt at all that the Admiral knew, too.

It was nearly dark when father and daughter came below. *Halimedes* lay at anchor in a dogleg cove, rocking gently with the tide. Through the galley port, Quade had a dusky view of the flat landscape beyond the water. Mostly sand and scrub. Still California, probably San Diego or thereabouts.

On his way through the cockpit, Arnie Stockton inhaled deeply and sighed. "Smells great!"

He still had an appetite, Quade noted, turning from the sink to watch Hallie, the Walther tucked in her waistband, fold her arms and lean against the navigation table to glare at him. "Have a nice little snoop?"

"Got a real kick out of your underwear," he told her. "You own stock in Victoria's Secret?"

Twilight hung thick in the cockpit so it was hard to tell for sure, but he could have sworn her wind-flushed face grew even brighter. A moment later the decking began to thrum and the lights to flicker on when Arnie Stockton cranked the generator Quade had seen earlier in a locker near the lavatory. Sure enough, Hallie's cheeks were as red as his windbreaker. With fury, not embarrassment.

When her father reappeared, she pushed off the navigation table and stalked aft with her nose in the air. The Commander watched her go, then turned a questioning eyebrow on Quade.

"She hates my guts," he explained.

Pursing his lips and nodding, Stockton poured himself a cup of coffee and carried it to the navigation table. Quade went back to the sink and his fruit salad. The water pressure fell to zero as the shower started. He shut off the tap and sighed. Arnie Stockton did, too, and looked up.

"Tell me about last night." He listened without comment or question until Quade told him how Hallie had faked him, maced him and beat the hell out of him with her tote. He grinned pridefully then. "She can take care of herself, can she?"

"Rest assured," Quade said.

"That's good." He looked down to run a finger along his plotted course and gulped his coffee.

The shower shut off, wet bare feet slapped on the decking, the aft cabin door shut with a slam. Quade turned the water on, his back to the chart table. Arnie Stockton's chin was quivering. Quade went on with his story, his hands steady. The Commander came into the galley to listen.

"Hallie said she wasn't tailed to the marina," he said when Quade finished.

"That's a six-hour jump on Conan. No more," he replied. "Once he's checked the airports, the highways, the train and the bus stations, he'll turn to the sea."

Arnie Stockton met his gaze directly. "I'm a wily old salt, Quade."

"Crossing the border won't stop him."

"I have something in the arsenal that will."

That, Quade thought, was an understatement. "What'd you do with the Camaro?"

"Pushed it off the pier."

The Commander winked and went to raise the table that was stowed beneath the port bunk. Hallie appeared in a peach cotton dress with a scoop neck and thin straps drooping down her arms. Her damp hair curled dark and wispy over her bare shoulders. No makeup, no shoes.

She didn't look tough. She looked soft, shy and unsure until Arnie leaned over the table between them and kissed her. She started to glow then. Her face gleamed, her rounded shoulders squared. Her brown eyes shone like liquid amber.

And she looked only at her father.

Quade turned away and served dinner on paper plates. Ham steaks, potato pancakes from a box of instant flakes, salad from cans of mandarin oranges and fruit cocktail. The Commander and his daughter sat on the port bunk, he poured coffee and took the starboard.

Halimedes rolled yearningly between the pull of her anchor and the swell of the tide, the deck underfoot thrummed steadily with the chug of the generator. When it cycled, the brass bunk lamps on the paneled bulkheads would dim. Not much, but enough to throw the bones of the Commander's face in sharp, skeletal relief.

Hallie didn't notice, even though she sat sideways on the bunk so she could watch him while she ate. She was talking when she wasn't chewing, making him smile, making him laugh. Her eyes would start to glow again when he did, so she'd try even harder to be funny.

She didn't know, Quade decided. Hadn't a clue that Arnie Stockton, who'd named his ship for her, who'd been thinking about her when he thought about the sea, had less than two years to live.

6

QUADE WOKE WITH A START a little before dawn, turned and bumped Arnie Stockton. The Commander's left shoulder hung off the bunk, his knuckles dragged the deck. He was snoring, asleep with his eyes opened.

He'd slept in the starboard bunk and Quade in the port so Hallie could have the cabin. Every muscle in Quade's body creaked as he swung his legs over the side and sat up.

The wind-up alarm on the ledge above the bunk said five-oh-seven. The Commander had set it for five-thirty, planning to be underway by first light. That gave Quade twenty minutes to call his own. He headed topside after a quick wash and a shave.

His head still felt like a split cantaloupe, but the salty tang in the air helped take some of the edge off. He stood near the rail breathing deep and watching the sun flirt with the low, fog-shrouded hills on the horizon. He'd slept a lot harder than he'd intended, an aftereffect of being concussed, could still feel his nerves jumping from the jolt of seeing Arnie staring at him like a dead fish.

Relief was a sharp taste in the back of his mouth. What a charming scene that would have been, telling the tough girl her old man had bought it during the night.

He rarely smoked before breakfast, but fished his hard pack out of his windbreaker pocket. Six left. He shook one out, lit it and repocketed the rest and his lighter.

"Early to bed, early to rise, huh?"

Quade glanced at Hallie. She held a white mug in each hand.

"Something like that," he replied, letting smoke drift from his nostrils.

Of all the times he'd been concussed, Quade couldn't recall his senses ever being this dull. She'd opened the hatch and popped herself through it without tripping him. It was his second jolt of the day and he didn't like it.

"You want this or not?" she asked.

Quade parked his cigarette in the corner of his mouth and took the mug she held in her left hand. His fingers were trembling.

She grinned at him, her amber-brown eyes gleaming with relish. "Still a bit rocky?"

"You do good work."

"From you that's a compliment. Thanks."

"Don't mention it." Quade took the other cup from her, stepped aside while she closed the hatch, then gave it back. *Ever again*, he thought sourly, inhaling as he pinched the cigarette from his lips between his thumb and forefinger.

She raised her mug and drank, eyeing him consideringly over the rim. Her hair was French-braided, which meant she'd been up awhile, her sweatshirt white with Desperately Seeking Sushi lettered across it in feathery pale blue script.

Quade smiled. She smelled good, had taken the time to put on perfume. Something light and flowery. Probably one of the Chanel scents.

Hallie glanced down at her chest, then at Quade. "You *do* have a sense of humor."

"Course I do. I took this job, didn't I?"

Exhaling through his nose, Quade walked back to the rail and flipped his cigarette over the side. Hallie followed.

"You might not be so shaky if you hadn't stayed up half the night watching for Conan."

"Dirty job but somebody had to do it."

"You want first watch tonight or second?"

Quade gulped his coffee. It was cooling rapidly in the chilly, damp air.

"I don't see any point in both of us staying awake," she added.

"Remember rule number two?" he asked. "Pick a side, any side, and stick to it?"

Hallie's jaw hardened. "Those are the Admiral's rules."

"Mine, too, tough girl."

"You were one of his brightest pupils, I'll bet."

"Once upon a time." Quade looked back at the rail, at the sun burning like an acetylene torch through the fog.

"What did he do to you?"

"Who says he did anything?"

"Your face, whenever I mention him."

"Perceptive little brat, aren't you?" Quade drained his mug and looked at her. "What did he do to you?"

"I asked you first, and I'm not a brat." Hallie caught the zipper of his windbreaker, gave it a tug and raised just her eyes to his face. "I'm not so little, either."

Quade's left hand flashed up and caught her wrist. "Don't bother. You're not my type."

She let her hand fall but raised her chin. No blush, just a determined glint in her yellow-flecked pupils.

"Arnie is dying."

"I didn't think you knew."

"Course I know—I'm not stupid. Besides, he told me."

"Maybe he'll get lucky."

"Arnie believes you'll give us till Ensenada, but I don't. Now hear this, Mr. Something Quade. I'm not going *anywhere*. I'm staying here with my father."

"We'll see about that, tough girl."

"You can't stand it because I beat you at your own game."

"This isn't a game. And so long as Conan's out there it isn't over. Not by a long shot."

"Says you. Arnie says he'll never find us."

"Then he's a bigger fool than you are."

For a second, Quade thought she'd toss her coffee in his face. She didn't, just drained her cup and jammed both hands on her hips. Coffee dripped past her cuffed white shorts raising gooseflesh on her calf. "There's two of us and we've got all the guns."

"I don't need guns and neither does Conan. Arnie's already got one foot in the grave. Keep pushing him, playing hide-and-seek and trying to outrun Conan and you'll put the other one on a banana peel."

That slowed her up for all of five seconds.

"Help us, then. Whatever the Admiral's paying you, I'll double. Triple," she said, when Quade snorted derisively and turned away from her. "My mother left me a fortune even the Admiral can't touch."

"You can't come close to his offer."

"It isn't money then."

Quade looked at her over his shoulder. She really was sharp. "No, it isn't money."

"Does revenge have any appeal for you? Don't take me back and he'll have a stroke."

"If I don't take you back I'll end up dead. If I leave you here, so will your dear old dad."

"Says you."

"You still don't get it, do you? You're the bait. Whoever hired Conan wants the Admiral and is using you to lure him out of Middleburg. That's why Conan killed Ferguson and Kazmerchek, because he *thought* they'd come to take you back. He'll kill Arnie, too, if he gets in his way."

"What d'you mean, *thought?*"

"The Admiral was inclined to let you have your fling. He sent Kazmerchek and Ferguson just to keep an eye on you."

Hallie's eyes widened. "And you believed him?"

"Incredible as it sounds, yeah."

"You don't look that dumb up close."

"I've got a couple of cards up my sleeve just in case."

"You better have an army up your sleeve."

Max was just as good as one, but Quade didn't say so.

"If you think for two seconds my grandfather intends to honor the agreement he made with you, you're a bigger fool than you think I am. He's raised giving it to you with one hand and taking it away with the other to an art form."

"That's not a news flash."

"Well here's one." Hallie jabbed her right index finger at him. "You even *try* to take me off this ship and I'll shoot you. So help me God, I will."

Snatching his empty mug from him, she spun around with a rubbery squeak on the ball of her foot and stalked away. Quade watched her. When she braced her foot on the right hatch door and bent over to fling open the left one, he let his gaze slide downward, then quickly away.

He wasn't concussed—he was nuts. She was the Admiral's granddaughter, for crissake. The hatch slammed and he felt it ricochet like a pistol shot inside his head.

Quade stood there wondering when the hell Hallie had gotten under his skin. He knew how, with her brass and her sass, starting that very first night in The Covey when she'd leaned over him and told him to tell her grandfather to go fornicate with the farm animals. He'd wanted to laugh, nearly had when he'd called the Admiral and told him.

"A rock club?" Old Iron Butt had bellowed. "What the hell's she doing in a dive like that?"

"It's just a guess," he'd replied dryly, "but I'd say she's rebelling."

Not surprising since the Admiral had kept her a virtual prisoner except for the year she'd spent in England. Even then he'd had her watched constantly. For a very long time Hiram Whitcomb had managed to keep his paranoia as well-hidden as his granddaughter. Quade hadn't known a thing about her until Max's phone call, and once upon a time he'd spent a lot of weekends in Middleburg.

Quade wondered where in that big old Georgian brick pile the Admiral had kept her stashed; wondered, too, what might have happened if he'd run into her in a hallway on a Sunday afternoon. She would have been on the dewy-eyed verge of making her debut in Washington society; he, a newly-commissioned, crew-cut second lieutenant.

Old Iron Butt would have keelhauled him, that's what.

In those days, nothing had made him hotter than milky-white pearls on a supple young throat. But that was ten years and two lifetimes ago. Now it took Reba and string bikinis. Or a smart-mouthed tough girl in fringed blue suede.

Revenge was tempting—nearly as tempting as Hallie Stockton and her amber-brown eyes. But this was his shot at redemption, at regaining all he'd lost. He wouldn't blow it, yet he felt the old familiar Dudley Do-Right yearnings that had made him such an easy mark for the Admiral in the first place.

Lousy timing, he told himself. That's all Hallie was. Lousy damned timing. Scrubbing both palms across his face, he clasped his hands behind his head and stared, unseeing, at the sun breaking through a cleft in the hills. *No guts, no glory. No ticket, no laundry. No grand-daughter, no pardon.*

"Dammit to hell," Quade muttered, wheeling away from the rail toward the hatch and breakfast.

He cooked it while Hallie glared at him from the chart table next to Arnie. Toast and oranges, omelets made from powdered eggs and leftover ham.

Hallie picked the meat out of hers. Arnie took a bite and almost cried. "How'd you do this with powdered eggs?"

"Held my mouth just right and spit in 'em."

Arnie guffawed. Hallie pushed her plate away and slammed out of the cockpit.

"I could use another hand topside," Arnie said. "I want to put as many miles as possible between us and this Conan character by nightfall."

"He'll come after us in a hydroplane if he can find one."

"I know that." Arnie wolfed another mouthful, chewed and swallowed. "But *Halimedes* is good cover. Thousands of sailboats go up and down the coast every day."

"He'll pay close attention to *any* ship heading south."

"I know that, too." Arnie finished his omelet and gulped his coffee. "What did Hallie try to bribe you with?"

"Her body. I declined."

"I thought she'd try money. She's an heiress, y'know."

"So she tells me, but I don't need the money."

"What *do* you need, Quade?"

"Something only the Admiral can give me. I'd help you if I could."

"I won't lie. I wish you would."

"Are you up to this?"

"I have been for twenty-four years. Hallie is my only child and I intend to hang on to her." Arnie smiled. "Too bad you work for the Admiral. I could like you."

"How long did you work for him?"

"I didn't. He tried to recruit me until he found out about his daughter and me. In the wink of an eye I was reassigned to Guam. Joanna ran away, I wangled leave and we were married in Honolulu. We had three weeks. Next thing I knew I was commanding a torpedo boat in the Gulf of Tonkin."

"That sounds like the Admiral," Quade said.

"It gets better." Arnie picked up an orange and began peeling it. "My ship blew up on routine night patrol. No mines, no torpedos, just a big boom in the engine room. I lost twelve crewmen. The rest of us were taken prisoner."

"What did you do besides sleep with his daughter?"

"I made her pregnant. The Admiral had visions of an annulment until then and an Annapolis grad from old money picked out for her. Jo wrote me about it. It was the last letter I ever got from her."

"So the only choice he had was to make her a widow."

"You're quick."

"I know the Admiral."

"I smelled sabotage, made up my mind to get out of the jungle alive and swapped tags with one of the guys I'd lost to protect myself. Smartest move I ever made. The VC were real interested in finding Commander Arnold Stockton."

"The old bastard was playing on both sides."

"He always has. Sometimes with an okay from the Pentagon, sometimes not. You wouldn't believe some of the stuff Jo told me."

Considering his own dealings with the Admiral, Quade thought he might but didn't say so.

"It was too much for Jo," Arnie continued quietly. "By the time I was released in a prisoner exchange near the end of the war, she was dead. Booze and drugs and God knows what."

"I take it you tried to see Hallie."

"*Tried* is the word. I spent two years in a *very* private hospital before I got to Middleburg. I wrote, but never got an answer. Two of the Admiral's goons met me at the gate, beat the hell out of me and promised to kill me if I ever came back." Arnie broke the orange in half and smiled ruefully. "They damn near did, too."

"How did Jo know so much about the Admiral's business?"

"She was his personal assistant."

Dumb move on the Admiral's part, but it hinted at a vulnerability Quade hadn't known Old Iron Butt possessed. It also hinted at a possibility that made the mouthful of omelet he'd just swallowed stick in his throat.

"In that case a very nasty thought occurs to me."

"I think I know what you're getting at, and I think Hallie may have hit you harder than you think."

"It makes as much sense as anything else."

"If the Admiral even suspected I knew too much, his goons would have finished me off when I showed up in Middleburg," Arnie insisted.

"Not unless you kept your identity and your destination a secret."

"Hell no I didn't. I told everybody at the hospital, everybody I could think of. I considered it insurance."

"I rest my case. Nam was one thing, but once you were stateside he didn't dare touch you. Too many people knew you were still alive."

"I suppose that's possible," Arnie said slowly.

And with just the right amount of thoughtfulness to draw a slow, satisfied smile from Quade.

7

BUT FAR TOO thoughtfully to suit Hallie.

She'd had a feeling the conversation might take this turn, so she'd hung around on the hatchway steps to eavesdrop. It was something she did very well, a skill perfected over a lifetime of living with the Admiral. She wouldn't put it past Quade to have made his disgusting comment just to get rid of her.

And it was time to call a halt to this. Taking a deep breath, Hallie entered. "Shame on you, tough guy. Scare tactics are strictly prohibited by rule number four."

"Hallie!" Arnie shot off the port bunk, so quickly he almost cracked his head on a beam.

"So's eavesdropping." Quade glared at her. "See rule number five."

"That's *your* rule number five. My rule number five says any player who catches an opponent breaking the rules may break any rule of her choice." Hallie smiled and folded her arms. "It's called the Rule of Tit for Tat."

Arnie wiped a hand over his grin and sat down. Quade gave her a frigid look. He'd tossed the red windbreaker on the bunk beside him and pushed up his sleeves. The talons and tail feathers of the eagle tattooed on his left forearm showed. So did a lot of muscle and a light growth of dark hair.

Her subconscious had been wrong about that. In the dream she'd had last night, he'd had lots of hair. Everywhere.

"This isn't a game," Quade said sharply. "This is real life and Conan is a very real threat."

"Baloney. You'd say or do anything to get me back to Middleburg. Even try to scare Arnie."

The only thing he hadn't tried so far was seducing her like he had in her dream. The incredibly *stupid* dream that had given her the idea to trot out her Mata Hari impersonation this morning.

"Carrying you back to old Virginie may be the only way to save your necks," Quade said bluntly. "This isn't an episode of *Flipper*. The good guys don't always win."

"Says you." Hallie lifted the carafe out of the coffee-maker and swung it over the table. "I say you're young enough and healthy enough to be a bigger threat to the Admiral than Arnie ever was."

"I'm flattered." Quade pushed his cup toward her. "But the Admiral wouldn't have to send me on a wild-goose chase to kill me. I live in D.C."

Silver Spring, actually. Hallie knew because she'd riffled his wallet the day before. What surprised her, so much so that the carafe slipped off the rim of his cup and sloshed coffee down the side, was that Quade volunteered it. He smiled at her and mopped the spill with a paper towel.

"The Admiral has only two types of acquaintances." Hallie put down the carafe and leaned her hands on the table. "People he hates and people who hate him. I think you fill both bills. And knowing Hiram Whitcomb to be the world's biggest welcher, I say he'd do anything to keep from paying you off."

"You're reaching, tough girl."

"So are you."

"Not any further than you are."

"All hands, this is the Captain," Arnie announced firmly, as he got to his feet. "Time to drink up and make fast for sail."

They did so in jig time. At least Quade did, while Arnie went topside and Hallie struggled with the double bunk in his cabin. She listened to Quade whistle "Are You Lonesome Tonight?" as he scraped, washed and put away dishes, and gritted her teeth in frustration. When he appeared in the doorway with a dish towel over his shoulder, she was still crawling around Arnie's rack trying to get the sheets straight.

"Need some help?"

Hallie looked up at him from the tangle of bedclothes in the middle of the bunk. "What makes you think that?"

"Hop off. I'll show you how it's done." He did, too, in half a dozen flips and tucks, then smiled. "Got a quarter?"

"Got any more dirty tricks up your sleeve?"

"One or two." His smile vanished. "You know what the great unwritten rule is, don't you?"

"Sure. There are no rules."

"Keep it in mind. And keep in mind that we'll make Ensenada tomorrow."

He left the cabin, and the temperature dropped about twenty degrees. Where her silly subconscious had gotten the idea Quade was even faintly attracted to her Hallie couldn't figure. When she heard the cockpit doors shut behind him, she sat down to think about whether or not the Admiral was trying to kill Arnie. Her hands shook. *Damn Quade, anyway.*

His theory made sense. The Admiral was ruthless and devious enough to construct such an elaborate scam. That he might have sent Ferguson and Kazmerchek to their deaths at Conan's hands just to snooker Quade made her blood run cold.

But if the Admiral had hired Conan to take care of Arnie, why involve Quade? Unless she was right and Conan was supposed to eliminate *Quade*, too. And that was an even scarier thought: two for the price of one.

The groan and rattle of the chain hauling up the anchor crawled a chill up Hallie's spine. If she went back, the Admiral would clamp a leash just as thick and just as heavy on her. She almost wished she was still a little girl, oblivious to the choke chain around her throat.

Ignorance had been bliss until she'd hit her teens and the Admiral had started jerking her leash. He'd misread her normal adolescent rebellion for defiance. He'd squelched every attempt she'd made to assert her independence, to find out who she was and what she wanted out of life.

And then Arnie had found her, shown her that her grandfather—the man she'd loved and trusted her whole life—had not only lied but conspired to keep her away from him. She still felt betrayed and angry. And used.

The trust she'd placed in the Admiral she'd shifted to Arnie. But if she found a way to outsmart Quade and stayed with him, she could be placing his life in jeopardy. Talk about a rock and a hard place. The devil and the deep blue sea, no-win scenario, backed into a corner. Any number of bleak little clichés fit.

And anything could happen between here and Ensenada. Conan could catch up with them, Arnie could make Quade walk the plank . . . or he could fall overboard. A shiver ran through Hallie as a shudder ran through *Halimedes*, her engines cranked over, her timbers creaked and she began to move.

God help her, she was thinking like the Admiral. Hallie held her hands out in front of her, saw they'd stopped shaking, picked up her sunglasses and went topside.

Arnie was at the wheel, Quade at the winch, ready to hoist sail. That he knew his way around a foredeck didn't surprise her. Nothing he did surprised her, except letting it slip that he lived in D.C. *So call me sometime,* she could shout down to him as she pushed him over the side. *We'll do lunch.*

The scrubby shoreline was slowly falling behind. Under power *Halimedes* was as graceful and just about as speedy as a duck on ice. Hallie gauged the distance at a quarter of a mile—an easy swim.

If you're going to do it, do *it,* she told herself, *before* Halimedes *clears the cove and Arnie gives the order to hoist sail.* Once the wind took her, *Halimedes* would take a leap like a jet off a runway. Hitting the water then would be risky, like hitting concrete.

Her hands were shaking again. Hallie tucked them in her pockets and sauntered toward the rail. From the corner of her eye, she saw Quade glance at her and felt her heartbeat accelerate. *Think ruthless. Think Ensenada.*

Chop just ahead, marking the convergence of the offshore currents and the calmer waters of the cove. The distance to shore was now almost half, maybe three-quarters of a mile. Still swimmable. *Fake a fall, make like you're going over. When Quade charges to the rescue, give him the old heave-ho and toss him a life jacket.*

The wind lifted, tugged loose tendrils of hair around her ears, the mouth of the cove slipped past at midships. Any second, Arnie would cut the engines. Hallie shook all over, her heart pounded in her ears. She clutched the rail and clenched her teeth. *Think* ruthless, *dammit. Think chain and anchor around your neck. Think you*

*and Arnie home free in Ensenada, Conan and Quade just
a bad dream.*

It was the wrong word to think. Smoky-gray dream
eyes almost black with desire flashed through her head,
then Conan's face, frozen in the rearview mirror for that
split second, Quade writhing in pain. Hallie felt her gorge
rise, swallowed hard and closed her eyes.

Fall. Now. Don't think, just do it. Her brain sent the
message but her body refused to comply. Her hands were
welded to the rail, her knees locked, her throat nearly
choked shut with panic and indecision.

"Hoist sail!" Arnie shouted.

Too late. The engines cut out, the winch whined and
spun, and canvas cracked as it unfurled. Too late. For a
heartbeat *Halimedes* floundered, then her sails snapped
fully open, her prow lifted and she veered, flying, into
the wind.

Whipping her head around, Hallie watched the flat,
sandy shoreline fall rapidly away, felt spray splash her
legs, blinked as it beaded on the lenses of her sunglasses.
So much for ruthless. So much for home free. No guts,
Quade had said to her. No guts, no glory.

"Thinking of throwing yourself overboard?"

Hallie turned and looked at him. She was glad she
couldn't see his eyes behind the mirrored sunglasses.

"Actually, I was thinking of throwing you over."

"Missed your chance."

"The story of my life," Hallie snapped, striding away
to join Arnie in the stern.

He lifted his right hand from the wheel and draped his
arm around her. Hallie laid her cheek on his shoulder and
tried not to cry. When she raised her head, Arnie was
looking at her soberly.

"Maybe I should try to raise the Admiral on the short-wave and play let's make a deal," she said.

"You can't deal with the devil, honey."

"Or Quade, either." Hallie frowned at him, still leaning on the rail and gazing out to sea. "I thought about tossing him over the side."

"Great minds think alike. But it occurred to me we might need him if this Conan catches up with us."

"We've got to stop for water sometime today, don't we?"

"We should. The tanks are low."

"He'll make his move then."

"He said Ensenada and I believe him."

Hallie studied her father's face. He looked a bit pale, a little gaunt with his hair sleeked back by the wind, but not at all gullible.

"How d'you know you can trust him?"

Arnie shrugged. "Gut feeling."

Near midday, they put in at a small marina Arnie knew. While *Halimedes'* tanks were filled, Arnie gave Hallie a list and a fifty-dollar bill and pointed her at the combination grocery and bait store. Quade trailed her along the quay.

"What's the matter, tough guy?" Hallie shortened her steps and let him catch up. "Don't trust me?"

He slid his hands into his pockets and squinted up at the nearly cloudless sky. "Not any farther than I can see you."

"There's the thanks I get for not feeding you to the fish this morning."

"If you're looking for thanks, look elsewhere. You should have left me in the parking lot in L.A."

"Oh, really?" Hallie stopped. "And where would you be if I had?"

"Dead, most likely," Quade replied with a shrug.

"You're damn right, dead. I save your life and you give me two lousy days with my dying father. Your compassion overwhelms me."

Quade faced her, sunlight glinting off his shades. "For you this is personal. For me it's just business."

"You're in this for whatever it is that only the Admiral can give you. That sounds pretty personal to me."

Quade didn't say anything, just looked at her. Hallie wanted to scream. Instead, she turned and stalked away.

Quade followed. Through the store that smelled like salt water and fish, through the checkout, wordlessly scooping up the three plastic sacks she filled. Hallie wondered what Arnie saw in Quade he thought he could trust.

He didn't say a word until they'd reached the boat, negotiated the hatchway and he'd dumped the sacks on the tiny galley countertop. Then he backed himself against the sink and folded his arms.

"Why didn't you leave me in the parking lot?"

Hallie had dropped to her heels to put a quart of milk in the compact fridge, then straightened and lifted her shades to the top of her head and looked at him. Sunlight glanced through the port, splashed little pools of wavering reflection on the paneled bulkheads and the planes of Quade's face.

"Because I'm not like you and the Admiral," she said. "I wouldn't have left my worst enemy in that parking lot. I admit I intended to, but when I saw Conan across Hollywood Boulevard, I knew I couldn't do it."

"No guts, tough girl," Quade said dispassionately. "No guts, no glory."

"Stow it," Hallie shot back disgustedly. "I may end up back in Middleburg, but I'll land there with my humanity intact. I won't be a monster like you and the Admiral."

"Don't hold back," he said, his voice as flat as his expression. "Tell me how you really feel."

"Go to hell." Hallie snatched her sunglasses out of her hair, jammed them over her nose and fled up the hatch.

8

ONCE *HALIMEDES'* TANKS were topped, the hoses disconnected and the lines cast off, they put out to sea. Quade made lunch, tuna-salad sandwiches with lettuce on rye. Arnie ate at the wheel, Quade at the boom. Since his presence on deck made hers superfluous, Hallie ate in the galley so she didn't have to look at him.

She went back on deck in a black maillot, one of Arnie's V-necked undershirts knotted at her waist and a big-brimmed straw hat. She'd bought it and one for Arnie, who had to be careful about too much sun in L.A.

In her absence Quade had ripped the sleeves out of his sweatshirt and cut his jeans off above the knee. He'd also rigged Arnie a shade out of a small tarp, but Hallie plunked the hat on her father's head anyway and told him he looked like Colonel Sanders. His raspy laugh made her throat ache.

The rest of the afternoon passed like a beer commercial—*Halimedes* skimming foam-capped water, the sky so blue and the canvas so white it hurt her eyes. Hallie spent the time with Arnie in the stern, in a green-and-white webbed aluminum chaise, watching Quade tack and trim sail, watching his well-defined arms and long, muscled legs turn a deep, sweat-gleamed bronze.

The man didn't even have the decency to sunburn. It was disgusting. So disgusting Hallie could almost hear John Denver singing "Aye, Calypso" in the background.

At sunset they put into a small cove cut nearly in half by a spit of land sprouting a dense growth of thin, reedy trees as tall as *Halimedes'* masts. While Hallie folded her chair, Arnie walked stiffly out of the stern. She paused to watch him, her pulse quickening at the trembling in his hands and legs. When the hatch banged shut behind him, the bronze god Quade leaned against the mainmast and cocked an eyebrow at her above the rims of his sunglasses.

"One foot on a banana peel," he said. "The other you know where."

Hallie dropped the chair before the urge to throw it at him overcame her, swept off her hat and her shades, unknotted her shirt and ripped it off as she walked to the rail. Glaring at Quade, she flipped the rope ladder over the side and said, "I'm going swimming."

She'd clambered after it and halfway down the rungs before he appeared above her, his hands spread on the rail.

"Not bright, tough girl. It's getting dark fast."

"I swim like a fish," Hallie snapped.

Which she'd learned to do because it was one of the few solitary things allowed her by the Admiral. At the waterline, Hallie kicked off *Halimedes* and swam until she ran out of air, about halfway across the cove, well past the tree-grown spit screening the schooner from view. Treading warm water and catching her breath, she bobbed lightly shoreward with the incoming tide, the sun setting over the Pacific a blinding silver glare.

Hallie turned her back to it, blinked to clear the spots from her eyes and missed a kick that dunked her for a second when she heard the thrum of an engine. She broke the surface almost instantly and held her breath listening. It *was* an engine—a big, powerful one, its growl thrumming up her spine. Her heart pounding madly, Hallie kicked herself around toward *Halimedes.*

Quade stood in the stern making an exaggerated thumbs-down sign. Hallie shot a glance toward the mouth of the cove, saw a flash of red fiberglass hull, sucked a breath and dove for the bottom.

She stayed down until her lungs felt ready to burst, then gave an upward thrust and surfaced just to port of *Halimedes,* in the black shadow of her stern. Pressing her thumb and forefinger to her eyes, Hallie gulped air through her mouth and listened. She could still hear the engine growl, lower and even slower. An inboard on idle, she thought. When it cut out completely, she sliced noiselessly through the water to her left.

Halimedes and the shoreward half of the cove lay in deep twilight and the shadows cast by the scrubby dunes ringing the water, the rest in gleaming, sunlit pewter. Keeping her chin just above water, Hallie slipped toward the ragged point of the tree-grown spit. Through bedraggled clumps of grass she saw a long, low-slung speedboat rocking in the mouth of the cove, the gold flecks in its red metallic hull glittering in the fading light.

The craft reeked of power. The driver reeked of menace.

It was Conan, in a red windbreaker and a white hat studded with lures. There were two other guys in the boat similarly rigged out. Just three guys out fishing with Uzis.

Hallie sank lower. They couldn't see her, and please God, they couldn't see *Halimedes* through the trees, either. She heard their voices but couldn't make out what they were saying. They were looking into the cove—Conan on his feet behind the wheel—trying to decide, Hallie guessed, if it was worth searching.

When Conan picked up a pair of binoculars, Hallie's heart almost stopped. He swept them slowly across the cove, at the waterline, not at a forty-five degree angle that might reveal the tips of *Halimedes'* masts above the trees. *So they don't know what they're looking for*, Hallie realized. *They're just looking.*

The guy riding in the rear seat—Sharkskin from L.A.—yawned and idly rubbed the barrel of his Uzi up and down his pant leg. Hallie shivered despite the warmth of the water. The boat rocked closer to the cove. Where was Arnie? Where was Quade? Where was the goddamn Coast Guard when you needed them?

The sun was sinking rapidly, the silver on the water fading into gray. Hallie's legs were tired. Conan lowered the glasses and talked to his cohorts. She caught two words—"shallow" and "sandbar"—felt a thrill of hope until her multilingual brain pointed out that she'd heard the words in Spanish.

Not significant, she decided, since it was the unofficial second language of California. Her gaze fixed on the boat, Hallie groped for the bank and a clump of soggy grass to keep herself afloat and rest her aching legs, touched something warm that grasped her back and stifled a scream.

It was Quade, soaking wet and bent on one knee on the bank to clasp her right hand in his left. He pressed his index finger to his lips, moved his grip from her hand to her elbow and pulled her close enough to loop his arm around her and lift her smoothly and silently out of the water.

Hallie had never been so glad to see anyone in her entire life. She clung to him for a moment, arms around his neck, then backed out of his loose embrace and gave him an okay nod. He pointed firmly at the ground meaning

"Stay put," and crept away toward the point of the land spit.

Hallie stayed, her bedraggled braid dripping down her back, muddy sand squishing between her toes. Over her shoulder, she looked at *Halimedes*, rearing dark and silent out of the water behind her.

There was no sign of Arnie at the portholes or on the deck a good fifteen feet overhead. She doubted Quade had had time to alert him, or to go below and find the Walther hidden inside her makeup bag. Fat lot of good a fifteen-shot clip would be versus a thirty-two-round magazine times three. Sixty-four times three, if Conan and his cohorts carried their Uzis with a second magazine welded to the first.

If the shooting started, they *might* stand a chance with the AK-47s Arnie had locked in the armory. *If* Arnie wasn't sick, *if* he'd had time to break them out and *if* she and Quade were aboard. Which they weren't.

If Conan decided to search the cove they'd need a diversion. Since she was the bait in the trap set for the Admiral, he wouldn't shoot her, and she might buy Quade time enough to get himself aboard and grab an assault rifle or two.

Hallie knew Conan wouldn't just take her and leave Arnie and Quade to go their own way, just like she knew Quade would never go for her plan. Deciding not to tell him, she started crawling toward the opposite bank. If Conan so much as twitched a finger toward the cove she'd fling herself in the water and start swimming for the speedboat.

She'd crawled within a couple of feet of the bank when the inboard roared to life and Quade clamped a hand around her ankle. Hallie glared at him, then reared up on her knees. Between two trees she saw Conan at the wheel of the boat cut a hard, one-hundred-eighty-degree turn. The prow lifted from the water as he punched the gas, and in a white-capped wake, he and his Uzi-toting pals sped away heading south.

Hallie went limp with relief until Quade grabbed her foot, gave her ankle a twist and flipped her over on her tush. Startled, she leaned on her hands and stared at him.

"Where the hell did you think you were going?"

"Back to *Halimedes* for your gun," Hallie lied.

"The goddamn boat is *that* way," Quade said, jerking a thumb over his shoulder.

"Oh, I—I guess it is," Hallie stammered. "I guess I got confused."

"*I* guess you were shooting for the Martyr of the Month Club." Quade pushed himself upright and loomed over her. "How the hell did the Admiral raise a goddamn Boy Scout?"

"Girl Scout. Get it right, will you?" Hallie slipped in the mud trying to stand, gave it up and fell back on her hands. "What was I supposed to do? Sit here and watch Conan and his pals make mincemeat of you and Arnie?"

"*Yes*, goddamn it. I'm a monster, not an idiot." Quade reached down, grabbed her right arm and yanked her to her feet. "I had a plan."

"Well thanks for sharing it. If I'd known I wouldn't have been so eager to make myself a diversion."

"Don't *ever* pull *anything* that goddamn *stupid* again." Quade bit the words at her, pulling her closer with each ground-out syllable. "You do and so help me God I'll drown you and tell the Admiral you fell overboard."

He flung her away from him and stalked toward *Halimedes*. Hallie trailed behind rubbing her arm. Not because it hurt—Quade knew precisely how much pressure to exert without doing damage—but to give herself something to do besides cry. She'd never felt so humiliated or so furious in all her life. Not even at the Admiral's hands.

"You said I was the lure, the bait in the trap to catch the Admiral. I thought—"

"Don't tell me." Quade spun around to glower at her. "You thought he'd keep you alive."

"I wouldn't be much of a lure dead."

"The hell you wouldn't. You've been on the loose three weeks, and so far nothing Conan has tried has budged the Admiral out of Middleburg. If he gets his hands on you, he'll start sending you home in little pieces."

Hallie didn't reply, just shivered and bit her lip. Quade made a disgusted noise and kept walking.

Hallie hurried to keep up, slipping along in the soggy grass a pace or two behind. When they reached the bank, Arnie was at *Halimedes'* port rail with an AK-47 in his hands.

"Thank God," he said shakily, as they stepped out of the trees. "That was close."

"Too damn close. We're lucky Conan decided this cove was too shallow and too sandy to fool with," Quade said, taking Hallie by the arm. "Now swim, fish."

He gave her a push into the water, dove in behind her, and swam a stroke or two off her right shoulder around *Halimedes'* stern to the rope ladder. Hallie went up first, acutely aware of Quade treading water below and glaring at her back as she climbed.

Arnie met her at the rail with the assault rifle looped over his shoulder by its strap and a blue towel. He wrapped her in it and pulled her against him, trembling despite the ferocity of his embrace. Or maybe because of it.

When Quade came dripping over the side, Arnie pitched him a second towel, a green one. "They'll be ahead of us tomorrow."

"Probably lying off in a cove," Quade replied, bending over to dry his hair. "That's what I'd do. I'd figure I'd passed you and wait for you to catch up."

The towel muffled his voice and the metallic rip of a zipper. Hallie heard it and turned out of Arnie's embrace in time to see Quade straighten with the towel around his shoulders, the Walther in his right hand and her makeup bag—her brand-new, watertight chintz vinyl makeup bag—in his left. He tossed it aside and leveled the nine-millimeter at her throat.

"Put the rifle down, Commander. Over by the hatch would be just fine. Then step back here."

Arnie spat a nasty curse but did what he was told, cupping his hands around Hallie's shoulders when he was finished. She reached up and twined her fingers with his. It was, she thought numbly, a toss-up as to which one of them was shaking worse than the other.

"I knew you wouldn't give us till Ensenada," she said bitterly.

"That's 'cause you're a smart little tough girl," Quade said, keeping his gaze fixed on Arnie. "Now let's everybody cooperate and nobody gets hurt. Give your daughter the key to the armory, Commander, then go take a swim while we lock it up."

"Sorry, honey." Arnie slipped the key into her hand and gave her fingers a reassuring squeeze. "I guess my guts were wrong."

9

FOR A BLIZZARD, THE STORM blowing snow across the Dulles International runways wasn't much, but the head cold raging through Quade's sinuses was a doozy. The bug had hit him when they'd boarded the plane in San Diego. The farther east they flew, the worse it got.

He'd popped two antihistamine tablets when they'd changed planes in Denver, but to no avail. Too many time and climate changes in too short a span. His throat felt like raw meat, when his ears weren't popping they seemed stuffed with wet cotton, and he couldn't breathe through his nose.

Every time he sneezed, Hallie smiled. It was the only sign that she was still alive in the seat next to him. She hadn't looked directly at him or spoken a word to him since he'd locked her in *Halimedes'* cabin for the night.

She'd turned around in the doorway and asked, "What's your first name?"

"What difference does it make?"

"I want to hate you," she'd replied. "Wholly, completely and *very* specifically."

"Frank N. Stein," he'd told her. "Quade is an alias."

She hadn't spoken another word since. He'd expected her to harangue him nonstop and make at least one attempt to escape. She'd had a perfect opportunity in San Diego while he'd been in the dressing room of the men's store where he'd slapped down his credit card for gray trousers, a maroon-and-gray sweater and a gray leather bomber. He'd given her the chance just to see what she'd do. She'd done nothing.

The 747 dropped lower on its final approach. Gritting his teeth at the nonstop popping in his ears, Quade slid Hallie a sideways look. She was smiling, but there were tiny white lines around her mouth that hadn't been there before and a pallor beneath the sun blush on her cheeks.

In the blue suede dress and boots she looked nothing at all like a rich little D.C. socialite. She looked sassy and brassy, her hair spritzed a foot out from her head and her eyes made up like a Kabuki dancer. When she was through with it, Quade hoped she'd give the dress to the Smithsonian.

The 747 touched down and rumbled its way to the outer terminal. Quade's ears gave up popping for ringing. Hallie didn't budge until he'd unfastened his seat belt; then she unhooked hers. She rose when he did, slipping into a blush-dyed silver-fox jacket rescued from her L.A. luggage, then just stood there, half turned away from him until he gave her a nudge into the aisle.

She didn't protest or pull away once the trolley delivered them to the main terminal and he took her left hand loosely in his right. There was just the tiniest shiver in her fingers when he led her through the building and outside again into the snow flurrying across the short-term parking.

When he unlocked and opened the passenger door, she slid into the black leather bucket and fastened her seat belt. Quade shut the door, walked around the car to open the other one, leaned inside long enough to start the engine and retrieve the ice scraper from the floor of the back seat.

While he cleaned the windows she sat staring at the station wagon parked nose-to-nose with the Mustang.

The tough girl he'd met in Los Angeles would have scrambled over the console by now, locked him out, rammed the gearshift into reverse and backed out of the parking space burning rubber. Maybe she was coming down with his cold.

The car was semiwarm when he pitched the scraper over the seat, took his wallet out of his jacket to pay the parking attendant and got in behind the wheel. Quade shifted into reverse and looked over his right shoulder to back the Mustang out of its spot. Hallie turned her head and looked out the side window.

Fifteen minutes later they left Sully Road for Route 50. She was still staring out the side window. The tail they'd picked up coming out of Dulles—two guys in a dark blue Lincoln Town Car—dropped back three car lengths.

The closer they got to Middleburg, the heavier the snow fell. Keeping them out of skids and ditches took most of Quade's attention until they turned off 50 onto the two-lane blacktop leading to the Admiral's compound.

From the corner of his eye Quade watched Hallie. Her knees trembled, her hands were clasped so tightly her knuckles were white. It dawned on him then that she was scared. She didn't scare easy and that stirred a pang of regret. *Look,* he wanted to tell her, *if there was any other way...* But there wasn't, so he lit a cigarette with the dash lighter and cracked his window.

"Would you stop for a minute?" she asked, her voice small and shaky.

Quade eased the Mustang off the road onto the verge of a freshly plowed drive. He pulled on the emergency brake, left the engine running and rolled his window down another notch. The Town Car cruised past and disappeared over the low hill just ahead.

Hallie turned sideways to face him, the warm air blowing out of the heater vents ruffling blush-colored fur around her chin. "Arnie gave you the Walther, didn't he?"

Quade took a drag of his cigarette and flipped the ash out the window. The smoke scratched his throat, the cold made his voice deeper than usual. "Why d'you say that?"

"He knew where it was. You didn't."

"You think I'm not smart enough to find it?"

"If you'd had time to look for it, yes, but you didn't. I think Arnie grabbed it when he went below and gave it to you while I was swimming, before Conan showed up."

"Why would he do that?"

"To get rid of me."

Quade glanced at her quivering chin and glistening amber-brown eyes. Where the hell she'd gotten the idea that she hadn't passed muster, that she'd failed to measure up to Arnie Stockton's expectations he couldn't imagine. The less she knew the better, but he could, Quade decided, at least set her straight about Arnie.

"While we were buying tuna fish, Arnie had a chat with the guy who runs the marina. Old friend of his. Conan had already been there, about two hours ahead of us. He had a picture of you and asked a lot of questions about the red-bearded Captain of a schooner named *Halimedes*."

Her eyes widened, then she flung her head away from him. "Why didn't he *tell* me?"

"One, he didn't want to scare you. Two, he didn't think you'd come along quietly with me. Three, he figured you'd be safest with the Admiral."

"Of course you agreed." She swung her chin around to look at him, dry-eyed, her voice steady. "What happened to rule number two? Pick a side, any side, and stick to it?"

Quade had hoped she'd forget that. He should have known better. Through the dusting of snow on the windshield he saw the dark blue Lincoln crest the hill coming toward them and turned on the windshield wipers.

"I didn't switch sides. Arnie did."

"Semantics. You agreed to help him."

"Why not? It dovetailed with what I wanted."

"Do you know where Arnie is?"

"Halfway to Hawaii." Watching the Town Car, Quade pushed in the cigarette lighter. "He intended to pick up a crew at the marina and head west as fast as he could."

Hallie's gaze flicked toward the Lincoln, slowing as it neared the Mustang. "To lead Conan away from us."

"Your favorite word, a diversion."

The lighter popped and Quade reached for it. At the last second, as the Town Car cruised past, he turned his head and caught Hallie's mouth with his. Her lips were cool and dry and parted in surprise. It was tempting, but Quade kept his tongue to himself, counted ten and pulled back, lifting his eyes to the rearview mirror. Hallie turned her head to look out the back window, sweeping her mane of stiff, finger-combed hair across his nose.

Just barely, Quade managed not to sneeze. The Lincoln's brake lights flashed and he smiled. Hallie blinked at him, touching her tongue to her bottom lip.

"They saw us," she said.

"I wanted them to." Quade straightened behind the wheel, the bomber jacket creaking against the seat back. "I'd much rather they tell the Admiral we were necking than talking."

"He won't like it."

Quade smiled at her and put the Mustang in gear. "I know."

She looked away from him and ducked her chin. The fringe on her dress parted, revealing a shapely length of thigh. Quade lit a cigarette and almost choked on the smoke. He was never sick, *never,* and this goddamn cold was really starting to piss him off. He glanced in the rearview mirror at the Lincoln coming up fast behind them. It slowed to a foot or so off the rear bumper and stayed there.

The compound gates swung open as he turned the Mustang off the road. The Lincoln followed, closing the gap between bumpers to mere inches. Quade ground out his cigarette in the ashtray, the back of his hand brushing Hallie's knee. She jumped and snapped her head toward him. Her eyes looked wet again, her pupils huge.

Her lips parted as if to say something, but she pressed them firmly shut and looked away from him. When he stopped the Mustang she gave the door a shove, swung her legs outside, paused and said over her shoulder, "Thanks for telling me about Arnie."

Then she rose out of the car and walked, back straight, up the steps and under the portico. The silver fox barely covered her knotted suede fringe.

The guy riding shotgun in the Lincoln followed Hallie, the driver waited for Quade to kill the engine and get out of the Mustang. They were both big. Not quite as big as Conan but close. So nice to be trusted.

A third linebacker-size tough opened the double front doors for Hallie. She walked past him, all blush-dyed fur and blue suede boots. The doorman's gaze slid after her. On the threshold Quade slipped, driving his elbow into the man's solar plexus. His eyes bulged and he doubled over.

"Sorry." Quade caught him before he fell, straightened him up and gave him a clap on the arm. "Wet shoes."

Quade stepped past him and saw Hallie, paused halfway across the green-and-cream parquet foyer waiting for him. He caught up with her, took her elbow and murmured in her ear, "Cheer up. At least you'll outlive the old bastard."

She said nothing, just squared her shoulders, shook her hair back and kept walking.

The Lincoln driver passed them to open the doors. Quade let go of Hallie and followed her into the library. When the second bozo who'd tailed them from Dulles stepped into the room and shut the doors, Quade knew for sure he'd been had. He'd suspected it since Arnie had told him Conan had beat them to the marina.

A pair of mahogany leather couches separated by a low, round table and a priceless Aubusson carpet had replaced the table set for two before the towering hearth. Another forest fire leaped behind the black net screen. Steam curled from a sterling coffee server on the table, gold-banded white china cups and an ashtray sat next to it.

The Admiral was reading the *Washington Post*. He looked up from the paper—not at Hallie but at Quade—took off his glasses and laid them aside with the *Post*. He didn't so much as glance at his granddaughter until she'd thrown herself down on the opposite couch and flung her jacket off her shoulders.

"You look like a strumpet," he said to her then.

"Nice to see you, too," she replied, swinging her right leg exaggeratedly over her left. "Does that mean you don't like my new look?"

"Go wash your face and change clothes while Mr. Quade and I conclude our business."

"Go fly a kite." Hallie shrugged out of the fox, helped herself to the coffee server and two cups. She filled one and lifted it to Quade without a saucer. "Just the way you like it, tough guy—black as your heart."

"Thanks." He took the cup in one hand, his cigarettes out of his inside jacket pocket with the other, sat down beside her and put the cup on the table.

Lipping a cigarette out of the pack, he cranked his lighter and bent his head. Over the flame he saw the Admiral nod. Quade snapped the lighter shut and squinted through blue smoke at the Lincoln driver rounding the back of the sofa to stop beside Hallie.

"Come with me, miss," he said, grasping her left elbow.

She tried, once, to wrench free, then glared at her grandfather. "Who the hell is he? My new maid?"

The Admiral ignored her. "Escort my granddaughter to her room, John."

"Very well, sir." He lifted her effortlessly from the couch, her arm stiff but the rest of her limp with shock.

She barely had time to shoot Quade a wide-eyed look of panic and reproach before John bore her away, her arm securely clamped in his ham-size fist. Quade tapped his cigarette in the ashtray and picked up his coffee. He blew on it and sipped, his hand steady despite the fury pounding in his ears. When the doors shut with a quiet click, he put the cup down and looked at the Admiral.

"So that's how you plan to keep her here. Strong-arm tactics. Very subtle."

"But effective," the old man replied mildly.

"She's home safe. That was our deal."

"You've gotten lazy working for Maxwell." The Admiral hitched his trouser leg and crossed his knees. "You left Conan alive. So long as he breathes, my granddaughter isn't safe."

"Conan wasn't part of the deal."

"Of course he was. I thought you understood that."

"I understand it now." Quade parked his cigarette in the ashtray. "You hired Conan to take out Arnie Stockton and me to take out Conan. You set the whole thing up to look like somebody was using Hallie to get to you."

The Admiral flicked a scrap of lint off his trousers, laced his fingers together atop his crossed knees. His knuckles were nearly as white as Hallie's had been. "Ridiculous."

"Damned clever. You even managed to snooker Max, and that's no easy trick. What's ridiculous is I fell for it. 'Course, you've always known the right carrot to dangle."

"I dangled nothing. You demanded the pardon."

"What the hell else would I ask for? Your granddaughter's hand in marriage?"

The Admiral's gaze narrowed. "Did you sleep with her?"

Quade wanted to hit him. Instead, he took a drag of his cigarette and snorted smoke through his nose.

"I can find out if you're lying. She was a virgin."

"Poor kid."

The Admiral's face darkened briefly, then he rose and tugged at his vest, a green one under a brown tweed jacket. "I believe our business is finished."

"Who do you plan to send after me?" Quade put out his cigarette, got to his feet and pointed his thumb at the second bodyguard standing by the door. "This bozo?"

"Consider yourself lucky." The Admiral eyed him coldly. "You've got your discharge, which is more than you deserve for such a sloppy job."

"And you've got your granddaughter, which is a helluva lot less than she deserves."

Quade moved to put his cigarettes back in his jacket, felt something cold bite behind his right ear and glanced over his shoulder at a .45 Magnum revolver pressed to his skull. He had to blink to bring the bozo's face into focus.

"See Mr. Quade out, Phillip," the Admiral said.

Phillip did, sliding into the passenger seat of the Lincoln once Quade was belted into the Mustang. John was already at the wheel of the Town Car, its engine idling. Quade started the Mustang and nosed it slowly down the long drive with the Lincoln on his bumper.

The gates swung automatically shut behind the black-and-silver ragtop. Quade stepped on the brake and the clutch, flipped on the left blinker but didn't make the turn until the Lincoln's doors sprang open and both John and Phillip started to get out.

The tail, another Lincoln, a gray one, picked him up on Route 50. When Quade turned into the secured parking beneath his building, it slid smoothly up to the curb.

In his third-floor apartment he stripped off his jacket and went to work. It took him less than five minutes to find the bugs and disable the tap wire on his phone. Nothing subtle or inspired here, either, which confirmed Quade's opinion of the Admiral's new henchmen.

Without his jacket, Quade took the elevator to the lobby and walked out the front door. It was still snowing. The guy in the gray Lincoln, almost a dead ringer for John and Phillip, rolled down the window as he approached. Quade tossed the bugs onto the seat beside him and spread his hands on the doorframe.

"Tell the Admiral to go fornicate with the farm animals," he said, then raised his right fist and punched the goon in the nose.

One knuckle popped, two bled, but it was nothing compared to the fountain spraying the steering wheel and dash. On his way back inside, Quade scooped up a handful of snow and pressed it to his throbbing hand. Despite the pain, he felt better. Much, much better.

No guts, no glory. No pardon, Quade decided with a grim smile, *no granddaughter.*

10

IT TOOK HALLIE ALL DAY Wednesday and most of the night to drag herself out of a crushing depression and her rumpled four-poster bed. She picked at the food brought to her on lap trays by John and Phillip and a third leviathan in a nose splint who wouldn't tell her his name and didn't respond to her insults. He looked enough like John and Phillip to be their triplet. Or a clone. Hallie called him Sousa. When she asked him how he broke his nose, he just glowered at her.

She cried when she wasn't sleeping and slept when she wasn't crying. She thought about Arnie and *Halimedes*. She dreamed about Quade. Dreams she either couldn't or didn't dare remember.

At four a.m. Thursday morning, she was in the library, a crystal old-fashioned glass full of the Admiral's brandy in her hand, staring at herself and the portrait of her mother in the marbled mirror. It seemed like a year, not just a week, since Quade had walked into The Covey in the gray silk Italian suit and ordered a Scotch and water, no ice.

Hallie stared at her mascara-blackened eyes, wrinkled lavender silk pajamas, and her mother's face smiling at her from the wall above the Admiral's desk. Joanna Whitcomb Stockton had blue eyes. Hallie's were brown like Arnie's. She had her father's mouth but her mother's hair, wheat blond streaked with brown and the same sharp chin, the Admiral's square jaw, and the intelligence to realize that if she didn't snap out of this she'd end up like her mother.

Hallie put the glass down and went upstairs. She took a shower, washed and dried her hair, gave herself a facial, a manicure and a pep talk. At eight-thirty, she put on periwinkle wool slacks and a matching sweater, taupe flats and tied her hair in a print scarf at the nape of her neck. She did her makeup, too, but her nose still looked red.

John, or maybe it was Phillip, sprang out of the chair outside her bedroom door and followed her to the dining room. The Admiral glanced up at her from the *Wall Street Journal* as she slid into her chair.

"Have you been crying?"

"No." Hallie sniffled. "I have a cold."

Gooseflesh shot through her. *Quade's cold.*

"John," the Admiral said to the bodyguard standing near the door. "Make an appointment with Rogers at Bethesda."

Hallie turned to watch him leave, then faced her grandfather. "I don't need a doctor and I don't need a shadow."

"After your ordeal, a good physical is in order. John is your punishment and your penance. Yet again, you've proved you can't be trusted."

Hallie picked up her napkin. "I'm twenty-three not thirteen. Adults leave home and live their own lives. They aren't punished and they don't do penance."

"We've discussed this before." The Admiral put down his gold-banded coffee cup, his voice harsh. "I've explained your position as my granddaughter and the necessity for precautions. You've chosen not to listen and to be irresponsible. You leave me no choice."

"My mother didn't listen to you, either, did she?"

"You're as stubborn and reckless as she was. That's why I have to protect you."

"The only thing scarier than John, Phillip and Sousa following me around is knowing you believe that." Throwing her napkin on her plate, Hallie got to her feet, slammed her chair against the table and stalked out of the dining room straight into John's hands.

"You have an eleven-thirty appointment," he said, catching her by the shoulders.

John took her to the naval medical center in the dark blue Lincoln, Phillip beside him in the front seat. He drove her back an hour and a half later. Phillip opened the car door for her, Sousa the front door of the house. Hallie rushed past them in a blur of blush-dyed fox, burst through the library doors and slammed them behind her so hard her mother's picture slid sideways on the wall.

"How *dare* you!" she seethed at the Admiral. "How goddamn *dare* you!"

He looked up at her from a stack of embossed, ivory vellum cards and a typed sheet of names. "Rogers phoned to tell me you refused the pelvic examination."

"You're goddamn right I refused!" Hallie flung herself across the room and spread her hands on the front edge of the desk. "What are you trying to do? Hang a rape charge on Quade so you can justify going after him like you went after Arnie?"

"If you've nothing to be ashamed of," the Admiral countered, "why did you refuse the exam?"

"The only thing I have to be ashamed of is you!"

The slap caught her off guard, snapped her head back but saved her, Hallie figured, from hyperventilation or fainting from sheer fury. Tears sprang in her eyes, but they were reflex, not emotion. The Admiral was on his feet behind his desk, his knuckles curled on its polished cherry surface.

"I've been wondering for the last ten years when you'd get around to doing that," Hallie said, her cheek throbbing.

"Go to your room."

"Go to hell," Hallie retorted, but she went.

Just inside her bedroom door her quaking knees gave out on her. She would have fallen if she hadn't grabbed the bedpost, screamed if she hadn't clapped a hand over her mouth. Claustrophobia clawed at her but she fought it with deep breaths. She would not panic. She would not despair. She would not roll over and play dead and she wouldn't snap. She'd escaped the Admiral once, and by God, she would again.

Flinging her jacket on the foot of her bed, Hallie went into the bathroom and looked in the mirror at the finger-shaped welts swelling on her right cheek. She probably should have sent John or Phillip for an ice bag, risked a bruise without it, but decided the reminder would be worth it. The pain would keep her sharp and sane, flaunting the bruise would be her revenge.

More than likely these were the same tactics the Admiral had used to break her mother's spirit. Hallie didn't remember her; she'd died two weeks before Hallie's third birthday. In a four-car pileup on the beltway, according to her grandfather. She hadn't discovered the truth until the Admiral had enrolled her at the exclusive Foxcross School, Joanna Whitcomb's alma mater, where the tragic death of such an illustrious alumna was still whispered about at faculty teas.

Maybe the Admiral realized he'd gone too far with her mother and maybe not. Maybe he figured if he couldn't break you and control you, he'd just as soon destroy you.

That seemed to be his MO with Arnie, who hadn't, as Quade pointed out, been a good little boy and gone away.

Hallie had no intention of being a good little girl, either. This time there'd be no help from Arnie, but she'd find a way to escape. To that end, she checked the bugs the Admiral had been routinely planting in her bedroom and sitting room since her fifteenth birthday.

They'd been moved around in her absence but not much. She left them where she found them; they might be useful later for misdirection. Then she checked her purse. Oddly, the cast-iron griddle was still in place beneath the false bottom, but the keys to her Mercedes convertible were gone. So were her credit cards and cash.

A knot of fury coiled in Hallie's chest, but she merely slapped her wallet shut and put it back in her tote. The Admiral knew as well as she did that it wasn't impossible to run without money. Just not as easy.

Twenty minutes later John knocked on her door to announce lunch. When Hallie entered the dining room, there was a manila folder next to her plate. She ignored it, spread her napkin as she sat down, picked up her fork and eyed her grandfather at the head of the table.

"Since my car keys are missing I assume John will be driving me to the Smithsonian."

"Not anymore," the Admiral replied curtly. "You tendered your resignation."

"Oh, really. When did I do that?"

"The day after you ran away to meet Arnie Stockton."

He made it sound like an accusation, not a statement.

"He's my father. I have every right to see him."

"He's an interloper and you have no rights other than those I choose to give you."

Hallie put down her fork, her stomach churning. "I wanted to join the State Department when I got my degree in languages but you nixed that. Accepting the Rhodes scholarship and working at the Smithsonian are the only things you've ever let me do. What am I supposed to do with myself now?"

"Since you can't be trusted past the gates, anything you wish within the confines of this compound."

"For how long?"

The Admiral shrugged. "I should think for at least the next two years."

Which was, barring remission, exactly how long Arnie's doctors had given him.

"In other words, the day my father dies I'll be free."

The Admiral lifted a crystal cruet and added more dressing to his salad. "Freedom is a relative concept."

"Relative to what?"

"Your cooperation." He picked up his fork and looked at her. "I have certain plans in mind."

"I'll bite. What plans?"

"I think it's time to find you a suitable husband. One with the proper breeding and background."

Hallie felt herself go cold all over. "I'm a human being not a brood mare."

"Considering your behavior with Quade, that would be difficult to prove."

There was no point in telling him there was no behavior to consider because he wouldn't believe her. She could submit to the exam and prove it, but she'd be damned if she would. Besides, medical reports could be faked, and Hallie had no doubt that Rogers at Bethesda knew exactly what the Admiral wanted and had already delivered it.

"Let me guess." She picked up her fork and speared a mouthful of salad. "You have the perfect grandson-in-law picked out for me."

"I have a candidate in mind, yes." The Admiral laid his fork on the edge of his plate. "I also want you to read that file. There are some things you should know about your lover. With good reason, Quade is not a talkative man."

Don't blush, Hallie thought, steeling herself against the heat she felt fanning up her throat. *He'll take it for guilt.* She took a sip of water and another mouthful.

"He is," the Admiral said, "a traitor to his country."

Hallie stopped chewing. "And you're a patriot?"

"He spent eighteen months in the Disciplinary Barracks at Fort Leavenworth," the Admiral went on, ignoring her comment. "He left an embassy satchel in the room of a Filipino whore. His lust came before his duty as a courier."

"Ooh, kinky. Did you know he's got a tattoo?"

"Yes. An eagle on his left forearm."

"Then you've never seen the one on his cheek?"

Hallie bit her tongue but too late. It took the Admiral a three-count to get it. When he did, his face turned an ugly, unbecoming purple.

"He'd better, by God, have protected you."

Hallie threw her napkin down and rose. "He brought me back here, didn't he?"

It was a great exit line if she'd ever heard one, so Hallie took it and herself to her room. Her big mouth had always been her best weapon against the Admiral, but she'd have to be careful she didn't hang Quade. Not that he didn't deserve it for bringing her back, but she felt guilty enough about leading Conan straight to Arnie.

She'd been the lure, all right, but the trap had been set for Arnie, not the Admiral. Quade must have figured it out when Arnie told him Conan had arrived at the marina ahead of *Halimedes*. That must have been when they'd hatched their plan to bring her back to Middleburg.

She and Arnie might be safe, but what about Quade? Was Conan stalking him now, or had the Admiral called him off? He was clearly out to nail Quade, which meant she'd been right on the money with her two-for-one theory. It also raised the possibility that the Admiral had flipped out. The parallels between the story she'd overheard Arnie tell Quade aboard *Halimedes* and her luncheon conversation with her grandfather were eerie.

Feeling the panic rising again, Hallie paced the room to calm herself. It seemed likely that Quade had at least made it out of the compound alive. The Admiral wouldn't bother to compile a file on a corpse. The thought made her shiver and chafe her arms.

She should have taken the file. Hallie cupped her elbows in her hands and wondered which part of the story about Quade was true. There was always a germ of truth someplace in the Admiral's lies. It made them more believable. The file might have given her clues. It might also have told her Quade's first name.

From riffling his wallet she knew he was six foot three, that he weighed two hundred and ten pounds, his address, his apartment number, his zip code and his date of birth, which made him thirty-two and a Scorpio. She knew everything but his first name.

It was a stupid thing to think about, but she'd wondered what his name was since she'd read E. H. Quade III on his Maryland driver's license, since she'd found the gold money-clip engraved with his initials in the change cup on the Mustang's console. Not that it mattered. Not that she'd ever see him again.

Hallie picked up her jacket, fished in the right pocket and withdrew the clip. She hadn't meant to keep it. She'd merely picked it up for something to hang on to, something for her hands to do besides beat the dashboard in frustration. He'd probably think he'd lost it, wouldn't miss it any more than he'd miss her; but at least she'd have something more substantial than his cold to remember him by.

She tried not to think about the kiss that had infected her, but the memory washed over her with a slow shiver. The tilt of Quade's head, the feel of his mouth, the taint of tobacco on his breath started her heart pounding.

The fact that he hadn't meant the kiss threatened to break it.

11

FOR DINNER, HALLIE PLAYED it cagey and claimed a headache. She doubted the Admiral believed her, but at least he sent up a meal. Once John collected her tray, she drifted restlessly across her bedroom to the French doors. The snow that hadn't melted off the balcony during the day had refrozen with nightfall. In the eerie glow of the outside lights, it glittered in the corners of the balcony and on the capped top of the balustrade.

So what if the Admiral had taken her credit cards? She'd memorized the numbers and expiration dates. To book a flight to Honolulu, all she needed was five minutes alone in the library on the Admiral's untapped phone line, a way past John, Phillip and Sousa, the cameras, alarms and motion detectors and transport to Dulles.

The alarms activated at sundown with the timer-controlled security spots. So did the motion detectors. There were two on her balcony and umpteen more strung across the lawn. Traversing the quarter-mile stretch between the house and the black iron fence would be like picking her way across a minefield. Too bad she couldn't fly. Or pole-vault.

Hallie tried but couldn't keep her mind on motion detectors and escape routes. Instead she thought about Arnie and her last day aboard *Halimedes*. She could still see the sun glinting on the wheel in his hands, the wind sleeking his hair. She refused to think about Quade and his sweat-glistened muscles. It was bad enough that she could still hear him whistling "Are You Lonesome To-night?"

She'd never forgive either of them for sending her back to Middleburg. She gave herself a week, tops, before being cooped up here drove her to a screaming leap off the balcony. How Arnie had survived four years in a bamboo cage and Quade eighteen months in the disciplinary barracks Hallie couldn't imagine, though now she knew what Arnie meant when he'd told her physical imprisonment wasn't the problem; the thing you had to watch out for was captivity of the spirit.

Maybe that explained Quade. Maybe his soul was still locked up in Leavenworth. Then again, maybe not. Arnie had been a prisoner a lot longer and he wasn't an emotional iceberg. Maybe it was the crime. It wasn't treason, no matter what the Admiral said. Quade would still be busting rocks for treason. Dereliction of duty, probably. The navy came down hard on that, especially in officers. Eighteen months sounded about right. So did a dishonorable discharge.

Maybe that was the thing only the Admiral could give him—an honorable discharge. To a tough guy who played by the rules, it would be important.

Hallie sighed and scratched her collarbone. Her sweater itched so she took it off, put on pink pajamas and a terry robe, switched on the right-hand lamp as she sat down at her dressing table and looked at herself in the mirror. Her eyes were puffy and glazed. Her nose was still red, the welts on her jaw had faded to four barely-there bruises. The bone beneath was sore to the touch.

Tugging the scarf out of her hair, Hallie picked up her brush and almost dropped it when her bedroom door opened. The Admiral appeared behind her in the mirror, a paisley silk dressing gown knotted over his shirt and trousers.

"How's your headache?" he asked, meeting her gaze in the glass.

"Better." Hallie pulled the brush through her hair, winced as it caught in a snarl and shut her eyes. When she opened them, the door was shut and the Admiral sat cross-kneed on the mahogany blanket box at the foot of her bed.

"I shouldn't have slapped you," he said.

In a quiet, almost humble voice that threw Hallie's senses on red alert. This was only the second time in her life her grandfather had come to her room, and the closest she'd ever heard him come to an apology.

His expression was unreadable, his face heavily shadowed in the dimly lit room. Only the two lamps at her bedside burned and the one on her table. Hallie switched on its companion, an ugly, outdated thing with a porcelain-ballerina base and a pink shade edged with gathered netting.

It didn't help. She still couldn't quite see the Admiral's face, but she remembered when he'd come to her room the first time, to forbid the removal of the god-awful lamps. They'd belonged to her mother, and even though Hallie hated them, he'd refused to allow their disposal.

The memory made Hallie shiver. "I'm very tired," she said. "I'd like to go to bed."

"In a moment." The Admiral stood, his hands in his pockets, and stepped into the light. There was a faint smile on his face. "We're having guests tomorrow evening."

"Guests?" Hallie almost dropped the brush again and gaped at him in the mirror. *"Here?"*

His smile vanished. "Of course, here. You know I don't go out."

"I also know why, and that you never let anyone past the door who hasn't been frisked and all but strip-searched."

The Admiral's formidable jaw went square and unyielding. "I'm willing to take the risk for your sake."

"Let me guess." Hallie tightened her grip on the brush. "The perfect grandson-in-law is on the guest list."

"I'd like you to wear these." He withdrew a gray velvet case from his right pocket, opened it and laid it on her dressing table. "With your saffron silk gown, I think."

A string of pearls with a diamond clasp and earrings to match shimmered on a bed of cream-colored satin. Gooseflesh crawled up Hallie's back. She'd seen the pearls that morning, in her mother's portrait.

"Cocktails at seven. Dancing at eight. A buffet supper at ten."

"You're opening the ballroom?" Hallie lifted her gaze to the mirror. At the Admiral's nod, she remembered the stack of cards on his desk that morning, the typed sheet of checked-off names. "How long have you been planning this?"

"Your hairdresser will be here at four." He ignored her question and turned toward the door. "Sleep well."

Hallie gave him fifteen minutes, ample time to reach his room and get into bed, then started for the attic. John sprang out of his chair when she came through her bedroom door. He made no effort to stop her, just stepped ahead of her at the end of the hall to open the attic door and turn on the stairwell light.

Two at a time Hallie sprang up the steps, flipped a switch and went straight to a bank of cedar closets built to store her mother's clothes. She pawed through dozens of designer originals snugly zipped into plastic bags, the scrape of the hangers on the rod making her grit her teeth. She found what she was looking for between a Dior dress and a Chanel suit, stepped back and stared at an off-the-shoulder saffron silk gown with a softly pleated skirt.

The Admiral had done everything but call her Joanna. Hallie hadn't any idea what had snapped in his head and caused him to confuse her with her mother, she only knew that he had. The question—did she gave guts enough to use it?—took her all of five seconds to answer.

You bet your life.

Lifting the gown by its hanger, Hallie draped it over her arm, shut the closet and made for the stairs. John followed, shutting off lights and closing the attic door.

"It's ten o'clock, miss," he said when they reached her bedroom. "I have to lock you in now."

"Since when?" Hallie hung the dress in her closet and looked at him over her shoulder. "I can't go anywhere. If I so much as touch a knob on an outside door or a window latch, I'll set off the alarms."

"I don't know why. Admiral's orders, starting tonight. If you need anything, knock. I'll be here all night."

"All right, John. Thank you."

"I'm Phillip, miss. Good night."

"Figures," Hallie muttered.

Removing the gown from its bag, she held it up to herself and smiled in the mirror on the inside of the closet door. It was a six and would fit, smelled faintly of cedar but had plenty of time to air out. It would be tea-length, even with the two-inch pumps she found that came close enough to matching. Too bad she had to wait twenty-four hours to gauge the Admiral's reaction.

Conscience and compassion held no meaning for him, yet Hallie felt a twinge of both when Phillip—or was it John—trailed her downstairs the next morning and she saw the Admiral sitting alone with his newspaper at the head of the mahogany dining table. Her emotions reassured Hallie that she had, in fact, landed back in Middleburg with her humanity intact.

She didn't know how she'd make use of the Admiral's confusion, only that she would if she got the chance—just as ruthlessly as he'd used her as bait to trap Arnie. She'd feel sorry for him once she was safely away. Maybe.

"Headache gone?" he asked, glancing up as she sat down.

"Yes, thanks." Hallie smiled. Feigned acquiescence was always a good way to start. "Can I help with things?"

"Staff has preparations in hand." The Admiral folded his paper and took off his glasses. "Your cold?"

"Much better."

"A walk might be just the thing. Put some bloom in your cheeks."

So she'd look good for the prospective grandson-in-law, Hallie thought, but kept smiling. "What a fine idea."

She went out after breakfast with John huddling along behind her in a sheepskin jacket. It was cold but the sun was bright, the snow on the lawn melting into icy puddles.

Her nose was all but running off her face when they came inside, but she'd pinpointed two dozen motion detectors, had half a path to the fence mapped in her head. And then it dawned on her—the house would be full of people tonight, the alarms and the motion detectors, at least at the front and along the drive, would be turned off.

Clever old Admiral. That's why he hadn't told her about the party until last night. He didn't trust her not to make a break for it. Even with such short notice, he probably still expected her to try. Which is exactly why Hallie had no intention of doing so, and why she hadn't tried to give Quade the slip in San Diego, either.

Rule number six was never be predictable. When her shot at escape came, she'd be ready. If she failed she'd never get another one, and Hallie didn't plan to fail.

She didn't plan to be nervous, either, but she was when she came downstairs at six forty-five in her mother's dress and pearls. For luck, she touched Quade's money clip, fastened to her bra inside her gown. The Admiral waited for her in the library in his dress whites and ribbons, took one look at her hair—pinned in loops at the crown of her head—glanced at Joanna's portrait and frowned at Hallie.

"Your hair is wrong," he said flatly.

"I can't wear a chignon." Hallie felt her skin crawl, tried to smile and not to shudder. "I have your jaw."

He raised an eyebrow, his gold braid and crew-cut, battleship-gray hair gleaming in the firelight. He looked perplexed. Then the doorbell pealed faintly and his expression smoothed.

"Come along," he said, offering his arm. "It's time to greet our guests."

The prospective grandson-in-law arrived in the third wave. Todd Sutherland, of the Chesapeake Sutherlands, old blood and even older money. No obvious signs of dissipation and not a dilettante, thank God. Pleasantly handsome with fair hair and hazel eyes, three years Hallie's senior, just embarking on a career in the Foreign Service.

The Admiral had at least made a stab at compatibility, for which Hallie was grateful. At least she'd get through the evening without being bored silly. When the hired orchestra began to play, the Admiral led her into the ballroom under the grand sweep of the galleried staircase, danced the first waltz with her, then handed her over to Todd.

The room filled gradually with the cream of Capitol Hill society. Senators and ambassadors, cabinet members and Pentagon chiefs—a testament to the Admiral's prestige and the power he held, even in retirement and seclusion. Crystal glittered in glasses and in chandeliers. Silver gleamed beneath sprays of orchids and mums. Champagne flowed.

"I think it's all wives here tonight," Todd murmured in Hallie's ear while they danced. "I don't see a single mistress. Or a married one, for that matter."

"No one," she replied, "would *dare* bring a floozy to Old Iron Butt's party."

Todd laughed. "My father has called the Admiral that as long as I can remember."

"I think the whole Pacific Fleet called him Old Iron Butt," Hallie said with a grin. "Just never to his face."

And wasn't it funny that Quade never had, she recalled, then resolutely pushed the thought out of her head. She was having trouble enough already, remembering that the last time she'd danced she'd been with Quade at The Covey. It was not a happy recollection. Evocative, yes. As calculatedly sensual in memory as it had been in fact.

"My dad graduated from Annapolis. He knew your father."

"Really?" Hallie kept her voice pleasant but went on yellow alert. It was possible the Admiral had put Todd up to quizzing her about Arnie. "I never did, you know. He was killed before I was born."

"Yes, I heard. Did you know our fathers were in competition for the hand of the fair Joanna? Very friendly, of course, since they were both officers and gentlemen."

Todd was trying to be charming, Hallie realized, trying to engage her interest. Still, she had a knot in her stomach and a bad feeling that she knew where this story was going to end.

"As Dad tells it, he had the inside track and the Admiral's blessing. He intended to pop the question the day your mother eloped with your father."

"How . . . ironic," Hallie managed to say around the knot that was now climbing up her throat.

"Personally, I'm delighted things worked out this way." Todd drew her closer and smiled. "I'd hate to be dancing with my sister."

"The Admiral had visions of an annulment," she'd overheard Arnie tell Quade. "An Annapolis grad from old money picked out for her."

Hallie had seen it coming, still she felt like Todd had hit her very hard with something very heavy. He twirled her around but her head kept spinning, her ears started to ring, and the chandeliers began to swing in slow motion.

Afraid she might faint or be sick down the front of Todd Sutherland's gleaming black tuxedo, Hallie closed her eyes and drew steadying breaths. The knot loosened its stranglehold on her throat and eased its way back to her stomach.

Exhaling the sick, shaky feeling, Hallie opened her eyes. The chandeliers had stopped swaying. Relieved, she lifted her head, gave Todd her brightest smile—and froze as her gaze locked on Quade, staring at her from the far side of the ballroom, the cigarette in his hand and his gray eyes smoldering.

12

HE WAS ALIVE. Not dead at Conan's hands. Alive and looking like he wanted to strangle somebody.

It was Quade's most endearing expression, the one Hallie had missed most. Never mind that she'd seen it only once, when he'd told her if she ever again pulled anything as goddamn stupid as making a diversion of herself he'd drown her.

Panic came hard on the heels of giddy relief, with the realization that he wouldn't be alive long once the Admiral saw him. If he hadn't already.

So much for relief. So much for Todd Sutherland.

"I'm sorry, Todd." Hallie smiled at him and backed out of his arms. "Forgive me, but I have to see someone."

"But, Hallie wait. I—"

That's all she heard as she turned away and launched herself across the ballroom. Quade intercepted her, swept her up like Fred Astaire and propelled her into the midst of the dancers. He wore a white dinner jacket and scarlet cummerbund, his trousers and bow tie were as black as the look on his face.

"How in hell," Hallie demanded, "did you get in here?"

Quade nodded at a distinguished-looking threesome smoking cigars and drinking champagne. "It pays to have friends in high places."

Hallie knew the congressman from Virginia, recognized an undersecretary and a member of the National

Security Council. "That ain't high, tough guy. That's exalted."

Quade shrugged. "Useful, if nothing else."

"What're you doing here? Besides tempting fate."

"I've come to take you away from all this."

His voice was typically deadpan, but something had set a match to the tundra Hallie was used to seeing in his gray eyes. He wasn't looking at her, didn't so much as glance at her. His gaze swept the room, seeking and still smoldering.

"Oh, very funny. I'm so sure you brought me back here just so you could rescue me. Hilarious. Hysterical. The funniest thing I've heard since—"

Quade looked at her, locked his gaze with hers. The tundra was about to burst into flame.

"Holy moley," Hallie breathed. "You mean it."

"You bet I do."

"When?"

"Any old time now."

Hallie's heart dropped like a stone. "How?"

"Same way we got out of The Covey. We're gonna walk out the front door calm and casual. Think you can manage that?"

"In my sleep."

"Without improvising?"

"I managed to in L.A."

"Be *sure*." Quade squeezed her hand. "There're at least six guys with guns in this room who'd love to blow my head off. I don't want that to happen. I'll be very upset if it does. Also very dead."

"I promise I'll do exactly what you tell me, the instant you tell me to do it," Hallie replied. "We walk out the front door and then what?"

"Get in my car and drive away."

The music ended with a polite smatter of applause. Quade released her, Hallie backstepped out of his arms.

"Drive away to where?"

"Dulles, for starters."

"And from there?"

"I'll tell you when we get in the car." His gaze slid from her face to her throat and back again, his hey-baby smile lifting one corner of his mouth. "Nice pearls."

"My mother's. So's the dress."

"Not bad." Quade's eyes lifted again, just a fraction, and one eyebrow notched. "Whose idea was the hairdo?"

Hallie felt herself start to shake. She'd be fine once they got moving and adrenaline kicked in. Her heart rate would pump up and so would her courage. She knew Quade knew it, too, and was trying to distract her.

"What's wrong with my hair?"

"Looks like you can pick up sitcoms from Venus."

Hallie laughed, not quite hysterically, but in the ball-park. The music started again, couples began to dance. Quade took her elbow and steered her off the floor.

"Are we leaving now?"

"In a minute." His gaze scanned the room again. "First we have to find the Admiral."

Hallie dragged him to a halt. Not intentionally, but because her knees nearly buckled. She'd been a lot braver in L.A. Just eight days ago, eight days B.C.—Before Conan. She was smarter now, smart enough to be scared out of her wits.

"Since when do the inmates announce a jail break to the warden? You've done time, you oughta know."

For just a second Hallie wished one of the guys with the guns would shoot her, then she thought Quade might. The flames in his eyes shrank to flickering pin-points.

"Oh, God, I'm *sorry*. I didn't think. I just—"

"Blurted it out." Quade's voice sliced through hers like a laser. "What's your point?"

"The Admiral thinks I'm my mother. That's why I'm wearing her dress and her pearls, that's why he intends to keep me a prisoner until Arnie's dead or I marry Todd Sutherland, the guy I was dancing with—the son of the Annapolis grad from old money the Admiral picked out for her. The Admiral will think you're taking Joanna."

"Even better." Quade smiled, applied pressure to her elbow and forced her to move.

"It isn't better, it's suicide."

"It's insurance. The Admiral is our ticket outta here."

Hallie glanced sideways at Quade. His jaw was as tight as his grip and the breakneck course he steered across the crowded ballroom.

"I get it now. He stiffed you."

"You said he would. I should've listened."

"So this is business." Hallie looked away from him, unable to keep the bitterness out of her voice. "Just when I thought you might be a human being after all."

"Well I'm not. I'm not a knight in shining armor, either." Quade shot her a brutal but mercifully brief glare. "Prince Valiant might risk his ass to save a twenty-three-year-old virgin, but I sure as hell don't."

"I am *not*," Hallie denied hotly, "a virgin!"

"Good for you. I hoped the Admiral was lying about that. But don't worry. I'll take you with me anyway."

"Oh, *thanks*. What if I don't want to go?"

"Not an option."

Hallie's adrenaline was pumping now. Streaking through her veins like high-octane ethyl. If Quade's intent was to fire her up past the point of fear he'd done a bang-up job.

He nudged her left to avoid a cluster of guests, then hauled her to a painful stop as a handsome couple with silvering dark hair turned into their path. A tall man in dress whites and ribbons, a woman shimmering in diamonds and rose satin, both smiling until they swung completely around. Their steps faltered then, their smiles turned brittle and tears sprang into the woman's eyes. Slate-gray eyes that made Hallie draw a breath and shoot a narrowed glance at Quade.

"You're breaking my arm," she said to him in a low, clenched voice.

No response, but she didn't expect one. He looked carved out of stone, caught in marble and caught in the act. Hallie studied Quade and then the woman, wondering which one would break first. She put her money on the bones in her arm.

She should have guessed it would be the man, a rear admiral by the braid on his sleeve. Without a flicker in his gaze or composure, he took the woman's arm and swept her straight across Hallie and Quade's path as if they were invisible.

Hallie felt him flinch, the vise on her arm relax, saw a ruddy flush climb up his throat. "You know those people."

"You could say that."

"Who are they? I mean, besides the rudest people I've ever seen in my life."

"Admiral and Mrs. Ellison Quade II," he said, stepping ahead to catch her wrist and tow her behind him.

"Admiral and—" Hallie stumbled on a shocked, indrawn breath and a rush of gooseflesh. "Your *parents*?"

Quade gave her a rueful glance. "You're quick tonight."

"In a million years I wouldn't have guessed your name is Ellison. Edward, maybe, or Ethan, or—"

"You're babbling." Quade let go of her wrist and turned to face her. "Stop it."

"I can't help it. I'm scared."

"At long last, but lousy timing. We're late for our rendezvous with Maxwell and the Admiral."

"Who's Maxwell?"

"One of the cards I told you I had up my sleeve. Be nice. He eats terrified virgins for lunch."

"I am *not*," Hallie repeated fiercely, "a virgin."

"But you're terrified and it shows. Scared is okay. In fact, scared is good. It'll keep you sharp." Quade took a step closer but didn't touch her, just trapped her gaze in his cold gray eyes. "Terrified will get me killed. And if you freeze up on me, you'd better pray to God they kill me."

"Oh gee, thanks. I feel *ever* so much better." Hallie's chin shot up. "Can we go now? Before I wet my pants?"

"Welcome back, tough girl. Stay with me now." Quade lifted her chin on his left index finger. "Who slapped you? The Admiral?"

There was no point in lying, no point in flushing, either, but she did. "You're quick tonight, too."

Quade tipped her chin another fraction to get a better look at the bruise. Probably to admire the handiwork.

"Listen up," he said. "Worst-case scenario is somebody'll start shooting. If I go down, Max'll cover you. My car's right outside the door, the engine's running. Clothes and plane tickets in a gym bag in the back, a gun in the console. The piece is mostly plastic, so you know what to do with it before you get on the plane. With me so far?"

"For better or worse," Hallie answered grimly.

"If there's a glitch, I'm gonna tell you to go. If I say it, do it. Don't stop for anything, not even to watch me bleed. I know you'd love to, but *don't*. I'll have Max send you pictures."

"Make sure they're in color," Hallie snapped, made edgy and waspish by his unnerving calm. "Why are you telling me all this?"

"So you'll know what to do if you have to." Quade made a light, half-moon stroke across the bruise on her cheek, then caught her hand. "Let's go."

13

THE THREE BIGGEST glitches Hallie could think of were nowhere in sight.

"I don't see my watchdogs," she told Quade. "Now that I think about it, I haven't seen them all night."

"The clowns who tailed us from Dulles? Don't sweat it. They're here someplace."

Hallie started to say that's why she was sweating it, but they stepped out of the ballroom into the foyer then, and she saw the Admiral. His face was waxen and shiny.

"He looks scared to death," Hallie murmured.

"He's furious," Quade replied. "Having a gun stuck in your kidney'll do that."

The man standing close beside and slightly behind the Admiral wasn't quite as dark as Quade, a bit taller and heavier. *Maxwell*, Hallie thought.

"What about the six guys with the guns?" she asked, glancing at the few guests drifting around the foyer.

"Taken care of or we wouldn't have made it this far."

Hallie decided she didn't want to know what that meant and suppressed a shiver as Quade led her up to the Admiral.

"Nice party, Hiram," he said. "Sorry we can't stay."

The Admiral turned to face them, his gaze narrowing at their joined hands, his jaw thrust forward like the prow of a ship. Behind him, Maxwell shifted accordingly.

"You'll end up in hell for this, Quade," the Admiral retorted. "I'll see to it personally."

"I promised if you set me up again I'd be back."

"I did not set you up. I told you the truth."

"If you'd told me the truth you'd'ave told me about Conan. You didn't."

"An unwise omission on my part." The Admiral moistened his lips. "I can still arrange a pardon."

"Too late. I'm stiffing you like you stiffed me. I'm walking out of here with the only thing you have left—your granddaughter. You're not only gonna let me, you're gonna be our safe passage. If your bozos try anything, you'll jeopardize her safety. You'll also leave Max no choice but to put you on dialysis for the rest of your life."

"For God's sake, don't take my daugh—er—my granddaughter. Don't involve her in this."

"I didn't involve her. *You* did."

At last the Admiral looked at Hallie. She tried to feel sympathy for him but couldn't; she only felt eyes on her back and an urgent desire to be gone from here.

"If you go with Quade you'll be in grave danger," he told her. "Even I may not be able to save you."

"I'm not afraid," Hallie said. "I'm in danger *here*—of losing my identity and my sanity. I'm going with Quade."

"With a traitor, you mean." The Admiral's mouth was a thin, bitter line. "I suppose blood tells after all."

This slap hurt far worse than the one on her cheek, but Hallie raised her chin and looked him straight in the eye. "I'll tell Arnie you said so."

"Her choice, Hiram. I have a witness." Quade nodded at Maxwell. "Don't even think about siccing the FBI on me."

"Don't worry." The Admiral made a fist of his right hand. "That's a pleasure I intend to keep for myself."

"I don't think so, Hiram." Quade smiled one of his frigid smiles. "You're nothing but a sorry, scared old man."

"We'll see who's sorry, mister." The Admiral's smile didn't quite reach his eyes. "Did you enjoy the reunion with your parents as much as I did?"

"Up yours, Hiram. Sideways. Now, if you'll excuse us."

Giving Hallie a nudge, Quade steered an unhurried course for the door. Maxwell herded the Admiral behind them. Still there was no sign of the triplets. Where the hell were they?

Hovering around Quade's Mustang and the dark green Jaguar parked behind it, Hallie saw, when they stepped outside—John behind the Jag, Phillip at the front of the Mustang, Sousa backing out from behind the wheel of the convertible, a last plume of exhaust evaporating from the tailpipe.

The smell hung thick on the frosty air, the ignition key and his nose splint gleamed in the well-lit dark beneath the portico. So did the steel bore of the Walther Quade withdrew from his jacket.

"Restart the engine and back off," he said.

They didn't budge until Maxwell drew a Beretta out of his pocket and used it to shove the Admiral forward. "Do as he says," the Admiral told them, and they did. Grudgingly.

"One more thing," Maxwell said. "The Admiral has agreed to join me in escorting Mr. Quade and Miss Stockton off the compound. I'll be driving him in my car."

This was clearly news to the Admiral. His bottom lip began to tremble. Hallie bit hers and looked away, shivering in the cold, and at last felt a pang of pity for him.

"I can't leave my guests," he said.

"You won't be gone long enough to be missed," Maxwell replied, "unless these three do something stupid. If that happens, you won't be returning at all."

"Don't worry, Hiram." Quade drew Hallie down the steps, giving John, Phillip and Sousa a wide berth and a good long look at the Walther. "I only told two or three of your oldest friends that you'd be out for a drive tonight."

"Open the gates," the Admiral ordered. "Tell the others to do *nothing*. Should any of the guests inquire, I've been called to the telephone and will rejoin them shortly."

The triplets hustled themselves into the house, Quade hustled Hallie behind the wheel of the Mustang. She knew why. In case of trouble, he'd have his hands free. She shut the door, fastened her seat belt and adjusted the rearview mirror to watch Maxwell escort the Admiral to the Jaguar.

Quade swung in beside her and shut his door, trapping the smell of exhaust and brittle winter night inside the car. Hallie put the engine in gear and both feet on the pedals, her hands clammy on the wheel and the shift lever.

"How long before they come after us?" she asked.

The Jaguar's headlights came on, outlining the huddled shape of the Admiral beside Maxwell in their backwash.

"Ten minutes, tops." Quade swiveled the heater vents toward her.

The warm air made her shiver as she took her foot off the clutch and nosed the Mustang down the sloping drive. In the glare of the Jaguar's lights Quade's face was nothing but shadows and sharp angles. His eyes moved from windshield to side mirror, the Walther steady in his right hand. Until now, Hallie hadn't noticed the adhesive tape wound around the knuckles of his first two fingers.

"But they won't follow us, will they?" she asked. "They'll follow the Admiral."

"That's the plan."

It was a brilliant plan. Awesomely simple and savage. Worthy of the Admiral.

"I thought you didn't like diversions."

"Depends on who's doing the diverting."

"Maxwell *will* take him back?"

"He shouldn't, but he will."

"The Admiral doesn't make empty promises." Hallie eased the Mustang through the first curve in the drive and glanced at Quade. "He meant what he said. If he doesn't have a stroke over this, he *will* come after you himself."

"That's the rest of the plan. That's why Max will take him back." Quade shot her a frown. "Alive and kicking, so stop looking at me like I'm Conan."

The ice crusted on the trees along the drive glittered in the headlights and blurred the tears burning suddenly in Hallie's eyes. She blinked furiously, stared straight ahead and refused to shed them.

So Quade wasn't Prince Valiant. So she was nothing more than a convenient red flag he could wave to enrage the bull. She ought to be glad and grateful he'd come for her, no matter what his reasons. She shouldn't feel kicked in the heart but she did, and so she told him, "I don't like being used any more than you do."

"Sorry, tough girl. Breaks of the game."

His flat tone of voice made her throat ache. "I don't think I want to play anymore."

"Don't worry. You won't have to for long."

The Mustang swooped through the second and last curve in the drive. The gates lay ahead, still solidly shut, their ice-coated black iron bars sparkling in the headlights and the halos ringing the carriage lamps atop the gateposts.

"Jesus Christ," Quade muttered disgustedly. "Everybody wants to be a goddamn hero. Pull up to the speaker."

Hallie's pulse raced as she eased the Mustang up to the right-hand post and Quade lowered his window. In the mirror, she saw the Jaguar come to a halt some twenty-or-so yards behind. The speaker crackled with static that rolled into the car on a blast of cold air.

"You're jerking with the Admiral's life here, fellas," Quade said into the grid.

"Give us a minute," came the reply. "The gates are frozen."

"Impossible," Hallie whispered. "They've been opened dozens of times tonight."

He nodded to her and said to the speaker, "You don't have a minute. Neither does the Admiral. Open up *now*."

There was no response, no static. Only silence as the speaker switched off. Dread washed over Hallie in a slow, sick wave and her heart shot up into her throat.

"Back up," Quade said.

Needlessly, for she already had the Mustang in reverse. Quade changed hands with the Walther, rolled up his window and gripped the door handle. Hallie stepped on the clutch and the brake, groped for the spring latch on the console. Quade would have to open the gates.

"The manual control panel is—"

"I know where it is. You've got the go-ahead. Remember what I told you." Quade pushed his left elbow on the console and shut it with a click. "No matter what happens just do what I told you and get the hell outta here."

"What if I don't?"

"I'll shoot you myself."

He looked like he had in The Covey when he'd backed her against the staircase and told her playtime was over. His voice and his eyes were as frigid as the darkness beyond the sweep of the headlights.

"I told you I'd do whatever you told me the instant you told me to do it."

"So you did. Then kiss me."

"For luck?"

"For the Admiral," he said, and swept his mouth over hers.

The kiss seared like dry ice, burning the shape of his mouth, the hard curve of his jaw into Hallie's senses. Then he swung away and kicked his door open. Cold sliced into the car as Quade bailed out, slammed the door and ran for the gates, the carriage lamps gleaming on his white-jacketed shoulders. Hallie held her breath until he'd ducked safely around the pillar, brushing snow off a feathery juniper.

Shifting into first, she kept both feet on the pedals and counted seconds in thousands. By touch she tripped the catch on the console, dipped her hand inside and withdrew the pistol, slipped it into her lap and kept counting.

One thousand thirty-five. Fifteen seconds more than it had taken Quade to crack the system in her beach house, and still the gates were closed.

"C'mon, tough guy," Hallie whispered urgently, lifting a searching gaze to the rearview mirror.

So far there was only the Jaguar behind her, darkness beyond the red glow of its taillights and the reach of the carriage lamps. Where the snow plowed off the drive had frozen in crusted ridges the blackness lightened. Beneath the trees it deepened and made her shiver. Hallie looked away, caught a flash of movement in the corner of her eye and raised her gaze again to the mirror—in time to see the Admiral snap around in his seat next to Maxwell.

A jolt of panic shot through her, but the gates were already swinging inward and Quade was sliding cautiously around the gatepost. There was no time to shout a warning, only a second to punch the heel of her hand on the horn.

Quade ducked, but too late. The bullet spun him around and sent him crashing into the juniper, denuding it of snow in a shower of diamond dust. There was no blood, no report Hallie could hear above the scream tearing up her throat. A second bullet struck the gatepost, sending brick and mortar chips flying.

Shoving the gearshift into park, Hallie unhooked her seat belt. When a third shot shattered the right side mirror, she did what Quade had told her not to—she froze.

She couldn't believe the Admiral's men were shooting at her; had always jeered at movie characters who turned into zombies or screaming meemies when bullets started flying. Hallie had never understood it, but she did when the right headlight exploded in a burst of broken glass— terror.

Enough to galvanize her and push her shoulder against the door, just as the Jaguar slammed into the back bumper. The impact snapped her neck, shoved her chin into the wheel, sent the gun in her lap skittering to the floor.

Dazed, Hallie straightened and shook her head, stared in the mirror at the Jaguar backing off and revving its engine. *"No!"* she shouted, but the chrome grill plowed into the bumper again and shoved the Mustang closer to the gates.

She was no match for Maxwell, and the silver ragtop was no match for the Jaguar. Hallie knew it. She knew, too, that if Quade could move he'd be on his feet by now.

He wasn't, which left her no choice but to do what he'd told her and get the hell out of here. Before Maxwell totaled the convertible, before she lost her nerve. She went, rocketing the Mustang through the gates. Tires screeching, the Jaguar followed.

Choking on a sob and tasting blood in her mouth, Hallie glanced in the mirror and watched the gates swing shut.

14

AT THE SULLY ROAD junction Maxwell fell back to lead the pursuit in the opposite direction. Caught in the horrific, slow-motion replay of Quade's backspin into the juniper playing over and over again in her mind, Hallie made a fishtailing turn off Route 50, only dimly aware of the farewell flash of the Jaguar's headlights.

When she reached Dulles, she parked the Mustang in the first space she found, switched off the lights, swept the gun off the floor, shoved it in the black nylon bag Quade had left in the back, shut the door and ran for the terminal. She hardly felt the cold or the wrench in her ankle when her right heel broke, just kicked off her shoes, scooped them up and kept running.

Hallie trashed the pumps in the first ladies' she came to, opened the bag, pulled out a denim jacket and jeans, a white turtleneck, socks and leather high-tops, a purple tie-on baseball cap, a single plane ticket and a folded sheaf of twenties. There was nothing else in the bag.

Hands shaking, she ripped out the fake bottom. Nothing underneath. The pockets held only the gun, a pair of sunglasses and a cosmetic bag. She unzipped it and shook out a hairbrush, toothbrush and paste, deodorant and soap, a compact of powdered foundation, blush, eye shadow, a bottle of Chanel No. 5.

There was no second plane ticket and nothing for Quade. The items in the bag were all for her, all her size. Quade had never planned to come with her; had either

known or guessed he wouldn't make it out of the compound.

The part of Hallie that felt betrayed wanted to tear the
sink out of the wall; the guilt and grief-stricken rest of her
wanted to throw her head back and howl like a banshee.
She didn't do either, just picked up the ticket.

"Honolulu," she read through a blur of tears.

Quade was sending her to Arnie. She had barely
twenty minutes to make the flight to San Francisco, a ten-
hour layover there, and the rest of her life to mourn.

She stripped, pulled on the jeans, sweater and jacket,
brushed her hair under the cap. Stuffing the ticket and
money in her pocket, she tied the high-tops, put on the
shades. Everything but the gun she zipped into the bag.

She could dismantle it but hadn't a clue how to hide
the cartridges from the X-ray machines and no time to
figure it out. Quade had wanted her to have it, but she'd
wanted him to kiss her for any reason but to provoke the
Admiral.

Hallie trashed the gun along with her mother's dress
and her panty hose, wadded the clip in a paper towel and
tossed it into the first trash can she came to on her
breakneck run to the trolley. She made the flight on the
last call and fell into her seat, chest heaving, ankle
throbbing, heart aching.

The plane was only a third full, which meant she had
no seatmates and all the coffee she could drink. It kept
fatigue and the shakes away. Hallie refused to let herself
sleep or think beyond the best way to go about finding
Arnie and *Halimedes* once she reached Honolulu.

Five and a half hours in a narrow coach seat left her
ankle stiff, but she managed to limp into the almost-
empty terminal. It was eleven-fifteen Pacific time. The
ticket counters were shutting down. Hallie waylaid a

ticket agent and found out the gate number for her Honolulu flight. On the same airline, luckily, so she didn't have far to hobble to find a closeby ladies', where she eased off her shoe and sock and frowned at her swollen and bruised foot.

Filling a sink with cold water and gritting her teeth, she swung her foot into it. When the water warmed, she refilled the sink with the hottest water she could stand. She repeated the process twice, dried off, put both socks on her right foot and laced her shoe up tight.

The contrast baths had eased the pain and swelling, the high-top would provide support. She'd need all she could get if Maxwell had kept his word and taken the Admiral back to the compound. Already he'd had plenty of time to throw out a net to haul her back to Middleburg.

Spending the night in the john was tempting but if one of the free-lancers the Admiral could muster with a phone call showed up, Hallie needed to spot him. Her ankle twinged when she turned toward the door but she could walk without limping. The glimpse she had of herself in the mirror reminded her of Linda Hamilton in *Terminator 2*, made her shiver and hitch the bag closer as she headed for the passenger lounge near the gate.

The wall clock behind the empty ticket counter said twelve-seventeen as she dragged an ashtray out of the smoking section. Swinging the bag and her foot on top of it, she settled into a chair that gave her a view of two entrances, a good long stretch of concourse and was close enough to the counter to dive behind it if necessary.

Knowing what her subconscious would dredge up if she slept kept Hallie's eyes open. She did nod off a time or two but jerked awake when her chin dropped onto her breastbone. She lost count of the times she walked around the lounge to keep her ankle from stiffening and her mind off Quade.

Eventually she'd have to think about him but not now. Maybe once she was safely aboard *Halimedes* she'd be able to face the snafu at the gates and her guilt. In the meantime she had to look sharp and get herself to Honolulu. It wasn't much, but it was the least she could do for Quade.

Her body was still on Eastern time and by six a.m. she'd been awake twenty-two hours. Every inch of her throbbed with fatigue. Three other people had straggled into the lounge, two men and a woman slouched in nearby chairs with their luggage. None of them paid any attention to her, but that, Hallie knew, could be deceptive.

She bet herself twenty bucks one of them would tail her into the bathroom, and held herself ready with the spray bottle of Chanel. A shot in the eyes would blind anybody who jumped her, but no attacker materialized. Hallie paid herself off with Quade's money, used the soap, the deodorant and the Chanel, brushed her hair and her teeth, washed her face and applied the makeup. The tie-on cap was giving her a headache so she left it off.

She felt better, smelled better, and didn't look made-up for a performance under the big top. Clever guy that Quade. He'd either read *Color Me Beautiful* or instinctively knew just what a girl needed to feel invincible. Too bad he hadn't been clever enough to keep himself from getting shot.

The thought gave Hallie a jolt of pain, this time in the heart. If she could believe the books she'd read to prepare herself for Arnie's death, only time would ease her grief. Maybe this was just a small taste of what she'd face then, but it didn't feel small. It felt huge and crushing.

Slowly but surely she was losing Arnie to Agent Orange. It didn't seem fair that she'd had to lose Quade just when she'd found him. And started to love him.

Oh, brother. Hallie shook her head, put on the shades and hooked the bag over her shoulder. He'd have a field day with that, give her a tough guy look and say something bitingly witty like, "What'er you, *nuts?*" Which wasn't especially witty, though it was plenty biting, still it made Hallie smile as she emerged from the bathroom and looked around.

A few more passengers had drifted into the area. The ticket counter was open, two agents behind it. A foggy, gritty dawn faintly pierced by streaky sun pressed against the glass-front wall of the terminal. So far so good.

Hallie turned toward the smell of coffee and an open snack bar. She bought a large and headed back to the gate, blowing on the steaming cup. It was seven-twenty. A thread of passengers with briefcases and garment bags formed a line at the ticket counter. The arrival and departure monitors flanking the clock had come to life. Her flight was fourth on the flickering green list.

Almost home free. Hallie felt relieved and hungry. Remembering glazed doughnuts tucked in paper doilies under glass, she did an about-face toward the snack bar and forgot how to move, how to breathe as her gaze fell on Quade.

Hands cupped around his lighter, the cigarette in his lips dipped into the flame, he stood no more than fifteen feet away from her near the glass front wall. When he flipped the lighter shut, caught the cigarette between the taped-up first two fingers of his right hand and tipped his head back to draw smoke into his lungs, she knew for sure he was live, not an hallucination.

He wore the leather bomber and maroon-banded sweater he'd bought in San Diego, ice-washed black jeans faded to a near shade of gray. A plane ticket folded into a paper envelope that matched Hallie's protruded from his pocket.

He exhaled, lowered his head and raised his hand to drag his fingers through his hair. In a beam of sunlight brightening through the glass, his face was the same color as the smoke drifting from his nostrils as his chin lifted suddenly and he saw her.

He blinked as a skycap pushing a luggage cart with a squeaky wheel passed between them. It might have been the sudden fade-out of the sun, or the fact that Hallie chose that moment to lift the shades off her nose, yet she thought she saw a flicker of his hey-baby smile as he bent his head to snuff out his cigarette and started toward her.

Dropping her coffee in a trash can, the black nylon bag on the floor and her sunglasses inside it, she ran to him, put her arms around his waist inside the gray bomber, buried her face in his chest and at last drew a breath.

He smelled like leather and cigarettes, not the antiseptic and sterile bandages Hallie expected. When his right arm locked around her, she remembered to exhale. When he laid his cheek against her temple, she sucked another breath that was mostly a joyful sob.

"Hey, tough girl," he murmured, the deep thrum of his voice in her ear making her quiver.

Much as she wanted to spend the rest of her life dug into Quade like a burr, Hallie took a half step back and looked at his face. His eyes were bloodshot, his chin and jaw blue with whiskers.

"Are you all right?"

"Don't I look all right?"

"Yes, but where—" Hallie faltered and swallowed hard "—where were you shot?"

"In the bulletproof vest." He wagged his eyebrows at her, twice. "I never crash a party without one."

Hallie blinked, backed up another step and punched him square in the solar plexus. Not hard enough to hurt him but hard enough to surprise him. His eyelids took a reflexive leap, his left hand came up to protect his ribs.

"You son of a *bitch!*" she shrieked. "Why didn't you tell me you were wearing body armor?"

"It's standard procedure." Quade frowned and rubbed his midsection. "I thought you knew the rules."

"I thought *you* were dead!"

He blinked, startled. "So you hit me."

"Yeah, so I hit you."

"I could hit you back."

"Go ahead." Hallie thrust her weight on one hip and folded her arms. "If you think you're big enough."

"Or we could kiss and make up."

"Just like that, huh?"

"No, just like this," he said, catching her chin.

It wasn't a dry-ice kiss. It was searing and provocatively slanted to tease her mouth open. He gave her bottom lip a feathery stroke with his tongue, the top one a barely-there scrape with his teeth and raised his head. Hallie didn't expect to see tundra in his eyes, but she did, realized what it meant and felt her stomach take a nosedive.

"Don't move." Quade spread his fingertips beneath her jaw. "Sharkskin Jacket from L.A. at two o'clock."

Oh God. He'd been on the red speedboat. If Sharkskin was here, so was Conan. Hallie fought the urge to look, the urge to run and forced herself to stay still. "Now what?"

"We get the hell outta here." Quade bent his head, appeared to be nibbling her mouth but murmured instructions. His lips moving against hers sent conflicting shivers of pleasure and terror up her back. "Plan A is the door and a cab. Plan B is down the escalator to Baggage Claim."

"How did Conan get here? Where did he come from? I watched all night and didn't see anybody suspicious."

"I don't know." Quade's right arm circled her shoulders and turned her around. "He wasn't on the jet I chartered in D.C. I checked every inch of it myself."

A smart pilot always did, which explained how Quade had made it to San Francisco. Hallie hadn't known he could fly, but wasn't surprised. Catching the nylon bag by its strap, she swung it off the floor. Quade took it from her, hitched it over his left shoulder and moved toward the closest exit.

So did two of the biggest men Hallie had ever seen, so big they blocked out the sun. Quade changed course toward a bank of escalators. The big men, Polynesian, by the brief glimpse Hallie had of them, followed with Sharkskin.

They weren't going to make it. She knew they weren't a half second before Conan, nattily dressed in a blue suit and shirt and a red tie, materialized out of the crowd. Quade knew it then, too, and brought them to a halt out of the mainstream of foot traffic. Conan approached, smiling. The two somber behemoths drew up close behind.

"Good morning, Mr. Quade. Miss Stockton." Conan's voice was deep, unaccented and pleasant. "Don't tell me you were thinking of leaving without me."

"Not anymore." Sourly, Quade eyed the giants looming over them like mountain ranges. "Isn't this over-kill?"

"I prefer to think of Nino and Sebu as insurance. You've led me a merry chase." Conan took a gold pin studded with jade stones in the shape of a pagoda from his pocket and offered it to Hallie. "I'd like you to wear this, please."

Hallie wanted no part of the brooch. She wanted to grab Quade's arm, click her heels three times and whisk them out of here. "I'd rather not," she replied.

"Please reconsider." Conan continued to smile. "My employer commissioned it for you."

"I don't give a damn who—"

"Put it on, Hallie," Quade cut in. "On your sweater, not your jacket. Right in the middle where he can see it."

It was the first time, the *only* time Quade had used her name. Hallie knew what that meant and did as she was told, careful not to touch Conan as she lifted the pagoda pin from his palm. She fumbled the catch, her fingers trembling.

"Thank you." Conan looked at Quade. "Keep in mind the detonator is in my pocket."

"Got it." Quade reached inside his bomber and withdrew the Walther from his holster.

Conan stepped closer to take it. So did one of the giants to block the exchange from view.

"Thank you, Mr. Quade. This way, please."

He led them toward the adjoining gate. One mountain walked beside Hallie, the other flanked Quade. Sharkskin took the black nylon bag from him and fell behind.

"What detonator?" she whispered to Quade.

"Your pin is an explosive. By the size of the stones about equivalent to three sticks of dynamite."

"Oh, *swell*." Hallie felt her stomach take another plunge.

"It's to keep me in line." Quade slid his hand under her elbow in time to keep her knees from buckling. "Do what he says and you'll be fine."

"Easy for you to say," she shot back. "You aren't wearing enough phony jade to blow up half this terminal."

The passengers crowding the lounge next to the gate they approached looked to be mostly Polynesian and Oriental. They stirred to life collecting luggage and children, as the loudspeakers came on to announce a nonstop flight for Manila.

Beside her, Quade made a noise in his throat and said under his breath, "Oh shit."

15

AND THAT'S ALL HE SAID, the whole long, wretched way across the Pacific and the international date line.

It was a lousy time to clam up. Hallie told him so in a whisper, mindful of Nino and Sebu slumbering behind them like dormant volcanos. Quade nodded at Conan, then kicked back his seat and shut his eyes.

He'd pulled the same trick on her on the way to Middleburg. Hallie recognized it but couldn't do a damn thing about it. She could sleep fitfully and she did, on and off, when she wasn't fuming at Quade or fretting about Conan.

He'd been waiting and ready for them in San Francisco, armed with the pagoda pin and the forged passports he'd given them before going through customs. Which meant someone had betrayed them—someone who knew Quade planned to spring her out of Middleburg.

Much as she wanted that someone to be the Admiral, Hallie couldn't see how it could be unless he was clairvoyant or damn lucky. But this didn't feel like luck. It felt inevitable, inescapable, gave her a cold, creepy crawl up the back of her neck.

The steamy heat of Manila warmed her, but not much. It was afternoon and it was Sunday when the jumbo jet landed. She took off her jacket and Quade set his watch as they shuffled through customs between Conan and

Nino and Sebu. Sharkskin had stayed in San Francisco, after he'd searched the black nylon bag and given it back.

For a wild second as a customs official examined its contents, Hallie considered telling him their passports were forgeries, then Conan stepped into her line of vision and slipped his hand in his pocket. She'd seen the detonator when he'd gone through the line ahead of them, a gold pillbox set with jade. Hallie looked away from him, the pagoda pin pulsing along with her heart at the base of her throat.

The inspector stamped their passports, smiled and told them in English to enjoy their stay in the Philippines.

"Fat chance," Quade muttered, swinging the black nylon bag over his shoulder and taking Hallie's elbow.

"You know where we're going, don't you?" she whispered.

"Haven't a clue."

"C'mon, tough guy."

"I'm pretty sure I know *who*. Not where."

"Okay. Who?"

"You'll find out," he said and clammed up again.

A white limo awaited them. Conan sat with the driver; Nino and Sebu faced Hallie and Quade in the back. The glass was heavily tinted, subduing the lush, tropical colors of Manila. It was also thick. Bulletproof, Hallie guessed.

Their destination was a marina where a flock of sea-planes rocked against their moorings. Quade asked in Filipino, received a nod, gave Hallie her sunglasses out of the bag and put on the pair she'd given him aboard *Halimedes*.

She asked for her cap in English and received another nod. *They're bilingual at least,* she thought, putting the hat on as she got out of the car.

The heat and humidity nearly staggered her, but Quade took her arm as they followed Conan across the quay and a bobbing, rope-railed dock toward a white plane striped in blue and maroon. Two hefty Filipinos guarded the open hatch.

The main cabin was lushly appointed with cream leather seats for twelve, and stifling despite the small fans ruffling her hair. The air-conditioning, she figured, wouldn't come on until the engines did.

Conan gestured Hallie to move to the rear. She went, heart pounding, and turned to face him where the aisle widened to make room for the bathroom and galley.

"You may remove the pin," he said.

Fear flashed through Hallie. Her gaze shot to the front of the plane where Nino and Sebu had Quade backed into a row of seats. He was peeling off his sweater, a muscle leaping in his jaw. She looked back at Conan and raised her chin. He had brown eyes, short-cropped brown hair and the biggest hands she'd ever seen.

"I think I'll keep it," she replied.

"Don't worry, Miss Stockton. Mr. Quade's fate does not rest with me but my employer. My instructions are to deliver you both."

"You don't work for my grandfather, do you?" Hallie took off the brooch and gave it to him.

"No." He dropped the pin in his pocket. "I must ask for your pearls, then I'd like you to step into the lavatory and remove your outer garments for examination. Draw the curtain if you wish to leave the door open and avoid heatstroke."

"You don't want to watch?" she taunted, lifting her hands to the diamond clasp beneath her hair.

"Thank you, no. I'm not a voyeur."

Hallie gave him the pearls and earrings, her sunglasses, jacket and cap, toed off her high-tops, tugged both socks off her right foot and handed them over.

"A nasty sprain," Conan said, eyeing her discolored ankle. "I may have something for it in the first-aid kit."

Hallie went into the bathroom, shucked off her jeans and sweater, handed them through the curtain and ducked back to the sink. She washed her throat, between her breasts and the sticky back of her neck.

Then she saw the camera, high up in the corner below the fan, almost obscured by the whirring blades blowing hot air on her. A tiny little thing nearly invisible against the muted blue-and-maroon textured wallcovering. Too late, she slapped her palm over Quade's money clip.

"If you please, Miss Stockton," Conan said, his upturned palm snaking through the curtain.

Hallie wanted to spit in it but didn't. *Not a voyeur!* she thought furiously, plucking the clip free of her bra as she stepped out of the lavatory and dropped it in his hand.

Even the Admiral had never put a camera in her bathroom. Hallie stayed behind the curtain out of lens range until Conan gave back her clothes, high-tops and an ankle brace.

She put the brace on first, then dressed, drew a deep breath and stepped through the curtain. Conan sat on the arm of a seat, her jacket thrown over its back, her hat upturned on his knee, her sunglasses inside.

"I'd appreciate some answers," she said to him.

"I can't give you any."

"I know the rules. It wouldn't be a violation to tell me where we're going and why."

"I don't play by the rules." Conan handed her the denim jacket and the cap. "Yours, Mr. Quade's or anyone else's."

Along with the sunglasses, there was a small slip of paper inside the hat. Hallie eyed it and Conan incredulously. "*A receipt* for the stuff in my pockets?"

"I'm a businessman, Miss Stockton. Not a thief."

That's not all you are, she thought, remembering Ferguson and Kazmerchek. Suppressing a shiver, Hallie moved up the aisle ahead of Conan and took the seat beside Quade.

"Nino will serve you a meal once we're airborne," Conan said, nodding at the mountain who'd taken Hallie's jacket and hung it in the closet beside Quade's bomber. "You are restricted only from the galley."

Then he disappeared into the cockpit with Sebu. There was another camera above the door that locked from the inside behind them. Nino signaled the guards on the dock to release the moorings, shut the outer hatch and went aft to secure the bathroom and the galley for takeoff.

Hallie studied his face as he passed her in search of something to distinguish him from Sebu. She found a tear-shaped nick, probably left by a knife point beneath his right eye, then put her thumb over the entry, "14K money clip, initials EHQ" on her receipt and showed it to Quade.

"Did you get one of these?"

He shook his head. The engines kicked over, rippling a shiver through the plane. Stale but cool air gushed out of the overhead ducts and ruffled his dark hair.

"He said he's a businessman, not a thief."

"So he is." Quade fastened his seat belt, saw it was twisted and unbuckled it. "And a damn good one."

"How can you say that? He's a *killer*, a paid assassin."

Quade raised just his eyes to her face, the sunlight slanting through the port winking on his sunglasses. "What do you think *I* am?"

Hallie had forgotten, felt her heart take a lurch that had nothing to do with the thump and bump of the plane. She knew why she'd forgotten, but she wasn't sure how, where or exactly when. Sometime, she was pretty sure, between the kiss he'd given her in the Mustang and the moment she'd seen him across the ballroom.

"You aren't like Conan. You're better than he is."

Quade gave a rueful snort. "Obviously I'm not or you wouldn't be here. You'd be aboard *Halimedes* with Arnie."

"That's not what I mean."

He stopped trying to straighten the belt and looked up at her. *Uh-oh,* Hallie thought. *Shouldn't have said that.* She saw it in her face, in her reflection on his lenses.

"I'm a monster, remember?"

"No, you're not."

"Yes, I am."

"Conan wouldn't have risked his neck to get me out of Middleburg. Not even with a bulletproof vest."

"Sure he would've. Probably not to bust you *out,* but he would've busted *in* for sure if somebody hadn't told him Max and I were going to do it for him."

"Who d'you think snitched?"

Quade shrugged. "Could've been you for all I know."

"Thanks."

"Rule number three—never trust anybody," Quade reminded her, then buckled his belt and looked away from her.

The plane cleared its berth, made a turn toward open water and gained speed for takeoff. Spray from the skis drummed the underbelly and sheeted across the port-hole.

Hallie strapped herself in and told Quade, "Conan says he doesn't play by the rules. Yours, mine or anybody's."

"Thanks for sharing that." He gave her a sideways frown. "But I sorta figured it out already."

"Listen, you old crab," she shot back. "I didn't enjoy being strip-searched on film any more than you did."

"Could've been worse. They could've worn surgical gloves and used petroleum jelly."

"Do you enjoy being disgusting?"

"Yes," Quade snapped, turning back to the port.

Hallie stuck her tongue out at the back of his head.

"I saw that," he said, but didn't look at her.

Neither did Nino as he came up the aisle and belted himself in for takeoff across from Hallie. She was sick and tired of being a pawn, but Quade wouldn't talk in front of Nino and she knew it. She decided to take another shot at him when the big guy got up to feed them, but Sebu came out of the cockpit to keep watch while Nino was in the galley.

Hallie wasn't hungry but ate anyway. Life with the Admiral had taught her never to pass up a meal. She didn't plan to sleep but she did, woke with her cheek stuck to the seat, her sunglasses gouging her temple, a crick in her neck and a headache pulsing between her eyes.

The direction of the sun slanting through the ports had changed. It was late in the day and they were heading south, she thought, but wasn't sure. The world had turned upside down once they'd crossed the equator. It was hardly a new sensation for Hallie, since she'd lost her bearings ten days ago when Quade had strolled into The Covey.

She yawned, saw Nino's seat was empty, peeled her face off the seat and glanced down the aisle. She couldn't see him but heard him moving around in the galley, rubbed her neck and leaned toward Quade. He was still gazing out the port. Over his shoulder, she saw blue water and green islands with white sand beaches.

"Where are we?" she asked sleepily.

"Sulu Islands, I think. Southern tip of the archipelago. More pirates and smugglers down there than fish."

"Pirates?" Hallie snapped fully awake. "What the hell do pirates want with us?"

"Criminals and thugs make great cover for rebels and insurgents." Quade gave her a brief look. "A very dangerous crowd. Tourists give the Sulus a wide berth. So does the law and the military."

"You've been in this neck of the woods before?"

"Aboard ship, yeah." Quade swung back to the port.

"Let me guess. Carrier duty."

Quade nodded.

"That's where you met the Admiral."

Another nod.

"So who d'you know among the rebels and insurgents?"

"Nobody. Not anymore."

"C'mon, tough guy. You said you know *who*, which means you know *why*. So does Conan. His instructions are to deliver both of us."

That surprised him enough to snap his head around.

"The Admiral told you why."

"He said you did eighteen months for leaving an embassy satchel in the room of a Filipino prostitute. I didn't believe him."

"You should have. It's the truth." Quade turned back to the port. "She was a great lay. The best I ever had."

"Is that supposed to shock me or shut me up?"

"What d'you think?"

Hallie thought it was supposed to do both. She knew he was getting surly, but she was getting desperate.

"The Admiral set you up to take the fall, didn't he?"

Quade didn't reply, just stared out the port.

"Admiral and Mrs. Ellison Quade II fell for it, too, didn't they? That's why they cut you dead."

Hallie knew he could move faster than a speeding bullet, yet she never saw him whip around. She didn't see his left hand come up under her chin, either, just caught her breath as his fingers clamped on her jaw.

"You're hurting me," she said.

"The hell I am. I know where every nerve in your face is. I know just where to press and how hard. I could break your jaw."

"Go ahead." He might as well, Hallie thought, since she had a feeling he was about to break her heart. She wished he'd take off the shades, yet felt glad she couldn't see his eyes.

"This isn't Beauty and the Beast, tough girl. I'm not some enchanted prince you can transform."

"Who says I want to?"

"You do, whenever I touch you."

"Then why don't you keep your hands to yourself? Or tell me what's going on. That's all I want."

He let go of her jaw, traced the tip of his index finger across her mouth. Hallie heard Nino's heavy tread behind them, felt the bottom drop out of her stomach and her lower lip quaver. Quade smiled. "Is it?"

"You aren't that irresistible," she said between clenched teeth. "We're losing altitude."

"Coming in for a landing." Quade straightened in his seat and gave his belt a cinch. "Buckle up, tough girl. From here on it's gonna be a damn bumpy ride."

16

QADE MEANT IT figuratively; still Hallie was surprised when the plane taxied up to its berth at a dock as modern as any she'd seen along the California coast aboard *Halimedes*. It was late afternoon, but a crane and a dozen or so dockhands were loading teak logs and bamboo into the hold of a small inter-island freighter.

A prosperous little place, Hallie thought, but it would have to be to afford the upkeep on Conan. No one glanced at her or Quade as Conan ushered them across the wharf into a Jeep Cherokee parked in a paved but sand-swept turnaround.

Through the back window, Hallie watched Sebu moor the seaplane. When the Jeep pulled away with Nino at the wheel and Conan beside him, she saw a slim, brown-skinned Filipino with an Uzi slung over his shoulder step out of the shadow cast by the crane's cab and light a cigarette. A not-so-subtle reminder that things weren't always what they seemed.

Hallie straightened beside Quade and watched the road narrow as it looped inland. A white-painted fence held back the forest of palms and bamboo that threatened to engulf the Jeep. There were potholes in low spots, humps and broken patches of pavement in places where the jungle strained the fence.

Most of them Nino avoided, those he couldn't jolted Hallie painfully up and down on the broad back seat until Quade released his seat belt and draped his left arm around her. Her first inclination was to shove him away, but she needed the ballast. Below his pushed-up sleeve, a sheen of sweat glistened in the light growth of hair on his forearm and the talons and tail feathers of the tattooed eagle.

It was more interesting than the back of Nino's head and less dangerous than Quade's face, so she looked at it and wondered how the tattooist had added the colors. She'd seen far more gruesome tattoos, yet couldn't imagine why a man who dressed like a *GQ* cover would have such a savage thing drawn on his arm.

The thought lifted Hallie's gaze to Conan. The sunlight piercing the jungle roof glanced through the windshield, splashed across his big hands at rest on his knees, his muscled neck and shoulders. She felt a chill wondering if he'd fractured Ferguson's skull as precisely and matter-of-factly as he'd written her receipt, as quickly and dispassionately as Quade had clamped the jawbreaker on her face.

Maybe that's what Quade meant when he'd told her aboard *Halimedes* that what you get ain't always what you see; maybe that's what the eagle signified. Snappy dresser but a predator beneath the plumage, a killer in an Italian silk suit. That's what he wanted her to believe. But Hallie couldn't, and knew why when the Jeep bounced into a pothole and Quade gripped her tighter to cushion her from the jolt.

Absorbing the shock with his own body wasn't the response of a killer; it was the reaction of an enchanted prince. Maybe she was fooling herself, but Hallie didn't think so. She thought Quade was fooling himself. Maybe she couldn't transform him, either, but she could love him. And she did. God help her, Beauty loved the Beast. Cold gray eyes, bloody feathers and all.

A house stood where the road emerged from the jungle, a sprawling white structure with a red tile roof surrounded by a lawn so green it looked fake. Flowers spilled over rock walls, peacocks drank from a fountain and preened in the trees. The house looked vaguely Spanish and sat smack in the middle of the immense lawn. Whoever built it knew the best place to hide was in plain sight.

The road cut a half circle in front of the house, then split in two. One fork hooked around a wing with latticed windows, the other curved out of sight toward a glimmer of blue water. Under a canopy of pine trees, Nino parked the Jeep. When Conan opened her door, Quade took his arm from her shoulders and slid out across the seat behind her. In the late but still-brilliant sun, Hallie blinked through her sunglasses at the carved teak front door of the house.

Conan's employer, the person who'd done murder and God only knew what else to bring her here, waited inside. Hallie supposed she ought to be frightened but she wasn't. She felt numb from the heat and fatigue and was damn glad.

She appreciated Quade's hand on the small of her back, as she followed Conan inside, her legs moving like they belonged to somebody else. Her ankle and the back of her neck ached, the headache she'd wakened with pulsed between her eyes.

The house was air-conditioned and cold. Generator powered, Hallie figured, since she hadn't seen any electrical lines. With the black nylon bag over his shoulder and Nino bringing up the rear, Conan led them down a wide central hall with a red tile floor into a room domed with skylights and scattered with rattan furniture.

Beyond open teak-framed glass doors that formed the outside walls lay a Japanese garden. Ceiling fans bolted to beams beneath the skylights pleasantly mixed the steamy air from outside with the icy draft from the hallway.

Leaving them just inside the doorway with Nino looming watchfully nearby, Conan went out into the garden. Hallie lifted her sunglasses to the top of her head and watched him disappear around a curve in a white gravel walk. His blue suit had scarcely a wrinkle in it. He was a fifty-two long, she figured, and didn't have a single sweat gland in his body.

He came back alone, crossed the room to a red-lacquered Chinese sideboard, emptied the contents of the black nylon bag and their confiscated belongings on top of it, stepped to one side and looked toward the garden. So did Hallie, as a woman moving as serenely as the breeze tinkling unseen wind chimes came around the curve in the gravel path.

Madonna might not kill for her figure or Kathleen Turner for her legs, but Hallie would. The mandarin collar and frogs at the shoulders of her red embroidered-silk dress matched the fringed parasol that hid her face. She collapsed it outside the door, leaned it against the frame and stepped inside. She was Eurasian and absolutely the most beautiful woman Hallie had ever seen.

"Ellison," she said, lifting her hand with a smile as she walked toward Quade.

She pronounced it "Ellaysan." For once in her life, Hallie wished she didn't have an IQ of 157. The connection between Quade's claim that he was pretty sure he knew who, not where, the embassy satchel and what appeared to be fourteen-karat gold tips on the woman's crimson nails seemed inescapable. Prostitution, Hallie judged, must pay damn well in these parts.

"Mai Lu." Quade took her hand and kissed it. "May I present Miss Hallie Stockton."

Hallie lifted her chin and met Mai Lu's eyes.

"How unfortunate that she looks like the Admiral," Mai Lu said, slipping her hand through Quade's elbow and drawing him toward a glass-topped table where a servant in a white jacket was placing a lacquered tray. "Let us have tea."

Her face in flames, Hallie watched Quade seat Mai Lu in a rattan chair padded in blue silk. Without waiting for an invitation, she followed them to the table, sat down with her elbows on the arms of her chair and looked Mai Lu square in her kohl-lined eyes.

"How unfortunate," she said, "that you're a whore."

Conan's head turned toward her and Quade's hands stilled on the curved back of Mai Lu's chair, but Hallie held her narrowed, sloe-eyed gaze unflinchingly. Her heart was banging in her throat, dread knotting in her stomach, but she'd be damned if she'd show it. Mai Lu could probably have her strangled with a single flick of one gold-tipped claw, but Hallie was through being pushed around.

"No longer. I am retired," Mai Lu replied, sliding a look at Conan over her shoulder. "I see why this one gave you such trouble."

"You want trouble, stay tuned," Hallie told her. "You ain't seen nothin' yet."

Her bold but empty threat brought a smile to Mai Lu's moist red mouth. "How much you remind me of your grandfather. Don't you think so, Ellison?"

"She's a real chip off the old block." Quade sat down across from Hallie, laid his sunglasses on the table and gave her a zip-your-lip glower.

She ignored him and asked Mai Lu, "Are you the brains or just the entertainment?"

"I am both," she replied, lifting a delicate china teapot from the lacquered tray.

She filled matching Chinese cups with green tea and gave the first one to Quade. *Figures,* Hallie thought. *A geisha to the bone.* She didn't like Mai Lu. She didn't like green tea, either, but she was thirsty so she drank it.

"I was most surprised to learn of your involvement in this very small and insignificant affair," Mai Lu said to Quade over the rim of her teacup.

"Not as surprised as I was when you walked through that door." He leaned back in his chair and wrapped his right hand around his cup. "I thought you and Rico and your left-wing pals planned to be in the presidential palace by now."

"Rico is dead." Mai Lu lowered her eyes and folded her hands in her lap. "The embassy satchel Admiral Whitcomb left in my room was a bomb. It exploded when Rico tried to open it. He was killed with seven of our compatriots. Our headquarters outside Manila was completely destroyed. I could not find enough of my husband to bury."

Somehow Hallie managed to swallow her mouthful of tea without choking. The wind chimes had fallen silent, a peacock screamed somewhere out in the garden.

"I'm sorry," Quade said. "I didn't know."

"Of course you did not. Your ship left the next day." Mai Lu sighed and refilled their cups, placing the pot back on the tray. "I wish I had died with Rico. I delivered the satchel and returned to Manila to keep my next assignation with the Admiral. He had no sooner risen from my bed when word of Rico's death reached me."

Hallie tasted something that wasn't green tea in the back of her mouth. Clamping her hands together between her knees, she looked at them through the glass table top. She wasn't fooled by Mai Lu's sob story, still she felt sorry for her. For herself and Quade, too, for this was no pirates' lair or smugglers' den, and Mai Lu wasn't simply a grieving widow.

Poignant as her tale was, Mai Lu couldn't quite keep the gleam of vengeance and revolutionary fervor out of her beautiful, almond-shaped eyes. She'd conspired with her dead husband and some unnamed bunch of left-wing radicals to overthrow the government and God only knew what else. Nothing penny ante, that was for sure.

The Admiral was a firm believer in payment in kind. Mai Lu hadn't told them what Rico had done to provoke retaliation and Hallie wasn't about to ask. Intercepted and murdered a bona fide courier, maybe, or knocked off a sailor or two on shore leave.

It was a fine line between rebel and patriot. In this case Hallie thought it was a coin toss. What was certain was that she and Quade were in deep doo-doo. The Admiral hadn't been kidding about grave danger. He'd told Quade he'd known about Conan, which meant he'd probably known or guessed about Mai Lu, too. She wondered if he knew who'd served them to her on a silver platter.

"It is nearly seven years since the Admiral murdered my Rico," she said softly, almost to herself. In the tabletop, Hallie saw her reflection shift toward her. "In all that time I have not seen Hiram Whitcomb, but I think I will be seeing him again very soon."

"I wouldn't count on it," Hallie replied, raising just her eyes from the cold tea in the bottom of her cup. "The

Admiral's pretty pissed off at me for leaving with Quade."

"He will come." Mai Lu lifted her hand and Hallie's chin on one fingertip. "He will come because he knows what I will do to you if he does not."

"Let me guess," Hallie said. "As soon as the Admiral shows up, Ellison and I will be free to go."

She pronounced his name "Ellaysan." She didn't mean to, it just slipped out. She felt pressure but no pain as Mai Lu's finger sliced across the underside of her chin. Hallie watched her smile, thought she saw Quade tense on the other side of the table but didn't dare move until Mai Lu took her finger away, the gold tip wet and red.

She bent her wrist then, pressed it to her chin and sucked a breath through her teeth. The salt in her sweat set fire to her skin and brought tears to her eyes.

"You should teach this child some manners, Ellison." Mai Lu rose, Quade already on his feet behind her to hold her chair.

"I think it's too late," he said, giving Hallie a shut-your-mouth-for-God's-sake-and-keep-it-shut look that neither Mai Lu, Nino or Conan could see.

"I suggest a spanking." Mai Lu spread her fingers on the beveled edge of the table and eyed Hallie consideringly. "I think this one would very much like to be in your lap."

Hallie decided she didn't dislike Mai Lu, she hated her. Almost as much as she hated herself for the blush she couldn't keep from climbing up her throat any more than she could keep from breathing. She felt Quade's eyes on her and ducked her head to watch Mai Lu cross the room to the lacquered sideboard.

She sorted the items Conan had placed there. The Walther to the right, her mother's pearls to the left, the spray bottle of Chanel to the right, Quade's lighter to the left. Those choices should have been reversed, Hallie thought, but she didn't say so.

"These things are harmless. You may take them with you to your quarters." Mai Lu picked up Quade's money clip and brought it to him.

He nodded as he took it from her and slipped it into his pocket. "Thanks. I thought I'd lost this."

"I found it," Conan volunteered, "clipped to Miss Stockton's brassiere."

Hallie ducked her head even lower and spread her fingers over her eyes. When Mai Lu laughed she squeezed them tightly shut and wished she'd stayed in Middleburg. When she snapped her fingers, Hallie started and jerked her chin up.

"Come along, little girl." She held out a hand to take the parasol Nino fetched from the garden doorway. "The sun is going down. It is time for children to be in bed."

Then she laughed again and turned down the hallway on Conan's arm. Nino waited for Hallie, so did Quade. She felt the cool sweep of his gray eyes as she pushed to her feet, but looked pointedly away from him, tugged her sunglasses out of her hair, jammed them over her nose and stalked after Mai Lu.

A white convertible limo waited outside. The top was down, Sebu was opening the front passenger door for Mai Lu. Nino stepped forward with the black nylon bag over his shoulder and opened the rear for Hallie and Quade. He sat beside her; Nino and Conan took the seat facing them.

Sebu followed the road through another patch of jungle no more than sixty yards deep. What sunlight pierced the tangle overhead flashed past on Mai Lu's red parasol.

The distant glimmer of blue Hallie had seen from the house was a bay almost as large as the one where the seaplane had landed, its surface glimmering in the sunset like newly polished pewter. Tucked into the elbow of the larger island was a much smaller one, hardly more than a cay completely surrounded by water. *Our quarters, I'll bet,* Hallie thought dismally.

At the dock a big, sleek cabin cruiser rocked. Conan went aboard first and straight into the wheelhouse, Sebu and Nino last after casting off the lines. It looked to be no more than a quarter mile to the island.

The engines cranked with a rumble Hallie felt through the soles of her high-tops. She sat with Quade on a padded portside bench facing the lowering sun. Mai Lu sat on the starboard side of the open rear deck, knees crossed, her parasol turning slowly on her shoulder.

The cruiser seemed unnecessarily large and powerful for such a short run. Or so Hallie thought until Conan cut the engines and Sebu and Nino got up to open lockers in the stern.

"Please." Mai Lu closed her parasol, rose and made a graceful gesture toward the stern. "I would like you to meet my children."

17

THE WHITE PLASTIC BUCKET of bloody chum in Nino's hand made bile rise in Hallie's throat. The one Sebu leaned over the side and thumped against the hull turned her stomach.

She wouldn't have made it to her feet if Quade hadn't taken her arm, but she balked when he nudged her forward. She had a shaky, cold-sweat suspicion what Mai Lu's children were and she wanted no part of them.

"C'mon, tough girl," Quade muttered in her ear. "No guts, no glory."

"If you say that to me one more time I'm gonna slug you," Hallie whispered, swallowing the vile taste in her mouth. "Don't let go of me, okay?"

"I won't," he promised, and he didn't. He stood solidly behind her in the stern, his grip on her elbow keeping her upright, even when Nino emptied his bucket over the side and the first fin surfaced.

Another dorsal broke to starboard as Sebu heaved pails full of mullet and Spanish mackerel overboard. A third shark sliced through the bloody foam on the water, submerged and resurfaced, its fin a glistening gray wedge. The engines kicked in to right the cruiser's drift, washing a plume of spray over the rail.

It was just enough to dampen the deck and put Hallie in fear of her footing. Reflexively she reached behind her, clutched a handful of black denim and thigh muscle.

Quade's fingers slid down her arm, between hers and made a fist.

The water was full of fins, more than Hallie could or wanted to count. Sebu and Nino pitched bucket after bucket of fish over the side in the cruiser's wake. The sharks followed. Hallie shivered and looked away, felt Quade's hand tighten over hers.

When the cruiser veered to port to circle the cay, Mai Lu turned to face them and smiled, her ebony hair gleaming blue in the fading sun. Her teeth weren't serrated, but ought to be, Hallie thought.

"I knew you were coming, so I have kept my darlings just a little hungry," she said. "There is an underwater net that keeps them in and the larger fish out, so they look forward to their morning and evening feedings."

Hallie glanced in the direction Mai Lu nodded, where the wrist and shoulder of the island drew close enough to make a shark gate feasible, yet still outrageously expensive. She doubted there was enough teak and bamboo in the whole of the Philippines to pay for half of what she'd seen so far, but alternative sources of income didn't bear thinking about. Neither did the loud splashing and thrashing off the stern. Hallie swallowed hard and fixed her attention on the cay.

It was bigger than it looked from the dock—maybe a mile long, perhaps a half to three-quarters deep—with more elevation than she'd thought. The far side was a sheer cliff, where a fine spray of rainbow mist arced above a cataract that plunged forty-or-so feet over the edge of the escarpment. In case Mai Lu decided to play fast and loose with the provisions, Hallie hoped it was fresh water.

As the cruiser rounded the cay and came windward of the big island she gave it a name. It wasn't original, but it was apt—Shark Island.

There was no boat at the dock the cruiser headed for, but that was no surprise. Sebu and Nino, with the black nylon bag over his shoulder, leaped nimbly over the side with the lines. Conan didn't shut the engines down, just cut them back to a dull throb and came out of the wheelhouse to stand behind Mai Lu.

Gingerly, Hallie took the hand Nino offered and hiked herself onto the dock. About forty or so yards up the beach she saw a red tile roof through a fringe of palms. At least they wouldn't have to thatch a hut, she thought, stepping out of the way as Quade came ashore and Nino gave him the black nylon bag.

"No, no, Ellison." Mai Lu made an impatient come-come gesture with her fingertips. "Your part in this is over."

Hallie's heart slammed into her rib cage, every drop of her blood drained to her feet. Quade swung the bag off his shoulder and held it out to her. She wouldn't take it, she couldn't. She couldn't move, breathe or think beyond how much she loved him.

"No guts, no glory, tough girl." Quade smiled a thin imitation of his quirky, one-sided smile, put down the bag and closed her chin between his thumb and curved forefinger. "Clean this up pronto, with salt water if nothing else. In this climate infections are dangerous."

That wasn't all that was dangerous, Hallie thought, watching him slip his right hand into his pocket. He caught hers in his left, pressed something into her palm and closed her fingers over it. Then he stepped back onto the cruiser and sat down on the starboard bench, the heel of his hands braced on the padded edge. Conan kept an eye on him until Sebu cleared the stern line and jumped aboard.

Hallie wanted to scream and cry, fall on her knees and beg, plead and grovel, but none of those things would do any good and she knew it. Most of all she wanted to open her hand and see what Quade had given her. Instead, she lifted her sunglasses to the top of her head and looked Mai Lu straight in the eye.

"Now go to bed, little girl," she said with a condescending smile. "You will find most of the comforts you are used to in the house. Mind the geckos, the small lizards that eat the mosquitoes, and do not wander too far into the jungle. Sebu has seen pythons, he says.

"Be sure to eat three meals a day. Nino will check on you in the morning and each evening. If you do not eat he will make you. I want you looking well and healthy when the Admiral arrives and I slit your throat in front of him."

Mai Lu nodded at Nino to loosen the bowline. He did so and stepped aboard. Sebu went into the wheelhouse, Conan remained on deck. Mai Lu sat down with her back to Hallie and opened her parasol, obliterating her view of Quade sitting with his shoulders hunched and looking astern.

Its engines grumbling in reverse, the cruiser backed away from the dock. Hallie opened her fingers and saw Quade's money clip in her palm. Her gaze flashed up at the cruiser, its prow swinging around in a froth of white water. Closing her fingers and kissing them for luck, she stuffed the clip in her pocket, dropped her sunglasses on the dock and toed off her high-tops. If her plan worked she'd need them. If not, Mai Lu would have a pair of hardly-used size sevens to give the next internee on Shark Island.

She peeled off her socks and the ankle brace, cuffed up her jeans and ran, heart pounding, off the dock and onto the beach. The cruiser had completed its turn and was making its way across the bay. But slowly, as Hallie had hoped it would, the better for Mai Lu to relish her triumph. She skidded to a halt on the hot sand at the water's edge, the beginning swell of the evening tide swirling around her ankles. She waited until Mai Lu looked back at her, then clenched her jaw.

"Relish this, bitch," Hallie said, and walked into the water.

Only half a second before Mai Lu, Quade sprang to his feet. This time Mai Lu didn't close her parasol, she threw it down still open on the deck. Conan didn't twitch a muscle, just stood with his arms folded over his abdomen watching Hallie wade into the gentle surf.

It wouldn't be for long and she knew it. So far there was warm sand underfoot, but once she lost bottom she'd have to swim. That would put her at greater risk from Mai Lu's children, but she was as good as dead, anyway, and so was Quade. If this didn't buy him a reprieve, at least she'd deprive Mai Lu the pleasure of cutting her throat in front of her grandfather.

Hallie kept one eye on the cruiser, the other on the water. It was so clear and so blue it hurt her eyes. She slogged on, wishing she hadn't left her shades on the dock. Her rolled-to-the-calf jeans were soaked to the thigh, the bottom starting to slant away from her.

A swell hit her in the midriff and pushed her back toward the beach, stumbling and wiping spray from her chin with the back of her hand. Over the whoosh of the waves beginning to rush ashore, she heard Mai Lu's raised voice but couldn't make out what she said. She did hear the cruiser's engines cut out and stopped waist-deep in roiling surf to wipe her stinging chin again.

That's when she saw the shark. About thirty yards ahead to her left, gliding toward her like a shadow beneath the water, almost eight feet long, its open jaws sifting the tide. Hallie didn't move, not even when a drop of blood from her chin, and then another, plopped into the water in front of her. She simply watched them spread like oil spots and undulate away from her with the reflux of the tide. *Oh, God,* she prayed, *let it kill me on the first strike.*

When the fin broke the surface, slicing a smooth, horizontal path in front of her, she drew in her breath and held it. When it changed direction toward her, idly, curiously, in no great hurry, she closed her eyes.

"Hey, you! Hey, ugly!" Quade shouted. "Come to Mama, you son of a bitch!"

Thwack, thwack, thwack. Hallie's eyes sprang open and she saw Quade, bent over the cruiser's stern, pounding one of the white plastic buckets against the hull. Beside him, Conan was doing the same thing with the other one.

No more than fifteen yards in front of her, the fin slipped beneath the water. Every cell in her body screamed *"Run!"* but she was paralyzed with terror. The cruiser's engines roared to life. Quade was bellowing, Mai Lu shrieking—probably with glee, Hallie thought numbly—then she felt a whoosh against her legs that all but staggered her, realized it was the backwash of the shark's tail flipping its body around and considered fainting until she saw the fin surface, moving vertically and at some speed away from her.

"Get out of the water!" Quade shouted. *"Now!"*

He was still beating what was left of the bucket against the hull. He'd hit it hard enough and often enough to pulverize it. The cruiser was churning rapidly toward shore in a spew of foam. Hallie swirled toward the beach, got caught by the surf, rolled and dumped hard on her back on the sand.

She didn't think she was hurt, just winded. Carefully, she levered herself up on one arm, then pushed woozily to her feet and stumbled around in time to see the cruiser bump up to the dock and Quade leap the rail.

Mai Lu had taken up her parasol, Conan an Uzi. Was he going to shoot her, Hallie wondered, or the shark? Quade cleared the dock and ran toward her kicking sand behind him. Hallie raked her wet hair out of her face and struggled out of the surf to meet him.

He whipped off his shades and went down on his knees in front of her. Hallie felt his hands quickly and efficiently explore her ankles and calves, move up to her knees. She was starting to shake, her teeth to chatter.

"You're all right, tough girl. Shake it off." Quade got to his feet, grabbed her arms and shook her hard enough to wobble the black spots swarming at the edges of her vision. "You had the piss scared out of you, that's all. Snap out of it. The Dragon Lady's waiting."

"That's who Mai Lu reminds me of," Hallie said, shivering but managing not to stutter. "The archvillainess in *Terry and the Pirates*, the Admiral's favorite comic strip."

"There's a marked similarity, but do us both a favor and keep it to yourself." Quade looped his arm round her and tucked her against him. "C'mon."

Hallie clung to him for support and warmth. In spite of the steamy heat she was freezing. She needed to get out of these clothes, stuff a pillow over her head and scream, but if Mai Lu's expression was any indication, she wouldn't be doing either one anytime soon.

The Dragon Lady stood on the dock by the cruiser with Conan and the Uzi beside her, both hands wrapped around her parasol. Its fringe stirred in the sultry shoreward breeze that was beginning to dry Hallie's clothes. Quade drew her to a halt in the sand beside the dock.

"You are not like the Admiral." Mai Lu stepped nearer the edge and looked down at Hallie. "You have courage."

"Where d'you think I learned it?" Hallie felt Quade's arm tense, but she wasn't about to back down now.

"If Ellison's life means so much to you, you may have it. For a time." Mai Lu's parasol began to rotate slowly. "Until I decide to cut his throat in front of you."

Then she turned away, Nino taking her hand to help her aboard the cruiser. Conan dropped Hallie's sunglasses into the black nylon bag, tossed it to Quade and followed Mai Lu. This time she didn't stay on deck, she preceded Conan into the wheelhouse while Sebu and Nino freed the lines.

Hallie watched the cruiser plow away in a wake of white water, full throttle toward the big island. There was thunder in the surf now, and in Quade's expression as he rooted through the bag for his cigarettes. Thinking she might have been smarter to let the shark have her, Hallie took a step away from him as he shook one out and lit it.

He didn't say a word, didn't so much as glance at her, just took a deep drag of the cigarette and watched the cruiser lengthen its distance from the island. Hallie watched Quade.

In the sun setting fire to the western tip of the cay, his features looked hammered out of bronze, his wind-tousled hair streaked with red. Hallie shivered and wished he'd do something, say something. He didn't until the cruiser had diminished in size by half, then he pitched his cigarette into the wet sand and swept her against him.

His gray sweater no longer smelled pleasantly of tobacco and leather—it stank. After her tumble in the surf, Hallie imagined she did, too, but she didn't care. She clung to Quade, who didn't seem to mind any more than she did.

"Who in hell taught you to play chicken with sharks?" he asked, catching a handful of her snarled, half-dry hair and pulling her head back to look at her.

"Nobody," Hallie replied, blinking up at his tight-jawed face. "I just—couldn't think of anything else to do."

"If you ever pull anything that goddamn stupid ever again, so help me, God, I'll—"

"Yeah yeah, I know," Hallie interrupted. "You'll drown me yourself and tell the Admiral I fell overboard."

"No, smartass. I won't marry you if we manage to get off this island alive," he said and kissed her. Hard, dragging her mouth up to meet his.

There was no tundra in his eyes when he broke the kiss, just the gleam of the fireball sun sinking into the sea, spreading long scarlet fingers tipped with molten gold across the beach and the surf foaming around their ankles.

"What?" Hallie breathed incredulously. "What did you say?"

"What, hell," Quade muttered and kissed her again, more gently this time.

Then he raised his head, threaded his fingers into the salt-tangled hair at her temples and pressed his lips to her forehead. His mouth shivered, and so did Hallie as she spread her hands on his chest and felt his heart slam against his ribs beneath her palms.

"You've got more guts than sense, you know that?" he said, the murmur of his lips shooting lush shivers across the nape of her neck.

"Who cares." Hallie sighed, savoring the rub of his fingertips against her temples. "It worked."

"I care." Quade gripped her elbows and backed her an arm's length away. "God help us both."

He didn't say he loved her but it was close enough. Hallie smiled at him, a lopsided, salt-crusted smile.

"Too late, tough guy. You should've strangled me when you had the chance."

He frowned and traced her bottom lip with his index finger. "Bite your tongue."

"I'd rather bite yours," Hallie said, touching the tip of her tongue to his finger.

He made a noise in his throat, his eyelashes swept half shut, and then he kissed her again, touching her with just his mouth. "Hold that thought," he said, a rough edge in his voice. "We've got things to do before the light goes."

Then he marched her purposefully toward the house behind the palm trees. Hallie looped both arms around his waist and laid her head against his chest, the stiff, goofy smile still on her face.

If Mai Lu had her way they were going to die, yet she'd never felt so happy in her life.

18

UNLESS HE COULD FIGURE a way off this miserable lump of sand—and fast—Quade knew they were going to die. If it came to that he'd kill Hallie himself, quickly and painlessly, before he'd let Mai Lu get her hands on her. And before that he'd make damn sure she died happy.

With any luck not on the beach. There ought to be at least one bed in the house, with a nice firm mattress where he could take her at length. If she still wanted him once she found out who he was ninety-nine-percent certain had conspired with Mai Lu to deliver the Admiral.

It was a natural if she thought about it, as he had all the way from San Francisco to Manila. He wouldn't volunteer anything, but he'd tell her if she asked him again. Part of him hoped she would, since it might save him from screwing up her psyche any worse than it was already. The rest of him hoped he could keep her distracted enough that she wouldn't think to ask.

There were two beds, doubles, in airy bedrooms connected by a bathroom with a separate tub and shower, two sinks and a private alcove for the toilet. Both opened through French doors onto a lanai scattered with rattan furniture that ran the back length of the small house. From the L-shaped living, dining and kitchen area another set of doors gave access to the garden beyond the lanai.

Quade stepped through these to have a look around while Hallie poked through the closets and drawers in the tall teak chests in the bedrooms.

On the rock wall edging the garden, he startled a gecko that scurried into a crevice and blinked at him with huge yellow eyes. He turned back to the house and saw Hallie in the doorway. When he stepped onto the lanai, she came out of the house and tossed a carton of cigarettes, his brand, onto the wicker table between them. Her eyes were nearly as big as the lizard's.

"I found this and clothes to fit you in the front bedroom. Enough for a week. Mai Lu clearly meant to bring you back. She was just jerking my chain to see what I'd do."

"Maybe." Quade wrapped his hands around the back of the chair in front of him. "Psychopaths aren't predictable."

"Tell me you never slept with her." Hallie hugged the dirty, sand-smeared front of her white sweater. "Even if it's a lie."

A lie would save her a lot of self-recriminations later but he couldn't do it, not with her eyes glimmering at him. "I didn't and that's the truth. The Admiral would've keelhauled anybody who sniffed around Mai Lu."

"There's a match made in hell." She shivered and looked away from him, her tightly-clenched arms relaxing a little. Her chin quavered, its underside an angry, fiery-looking red Quade didn't like.

"C'mere." He reached for her hand over the table, led her into the bathroom and sat her down on the closed toilet lid. She clamped her hands between her knees while he dug through the medicine cabinet, looked up at him when he came toward her with hydrogen peroxide, Merthiolate and cotton balls. "This is gonna hurt."

"There isn't much that's happened to me in the last ten days that hasn't, one way or another."

She said it matter-of-factly, not bitterly. A real tough girl, except for the reflexive clamp of her hands on his when he tried to tug her sweater out of her waistband.

"This needs to come off. Once I've cleaned your chin I don't want any more dirt in it. Besides," he murmured against her mouth, leaning forward to kiss her while he freed the filthy sweater from her jeans, "I'm gonna see all of you later."

She let go of his wrists then, let him pull her arms out of the sleeves and ease, not peel, the sweater over her head. She had round little breasts and about half a pound of sand inside her lacy white bra. Quade went down on his knees and kissed her breastbone. Hallie shivered.

"Where'd you find my money clip?" He rocked back on his heels and soaked a cotton ball with peroxide. "In the car?"

"Yes. I didn't mean to keep it. I—" She sucked air through her teeth and bit her lip when the cotton touched her chin. "It was just something to hold on to. I didn't mean to take it."

"It's okay. I gave it back to you, didn't I?"

He dabbed her chin with peroxide until it bled, soaked another cotton ball, told her to press it as tight as she could against her chin and hold it there. Then he got up and turned on the shower. In the closet in the bedroom Mai Lu had prepared for Hallie, the back one that opened onto the lanai, he found shampoo and soap, towels and a robe.

The bathroom was pleasantly steamed, Hallie's skin alluringly flushed. Quade felt himself stir looking at her, took the cotton ball away and stood her up. He kissed her, unsnapped the hook on her bra, cupped her shoulder blades in his palms and lifted his head. Her bra gaped enough to show him her nipples stiffening beneath a slow crawl of gooseflesh across her collarbones.

"I have to scope out the island while there's light enough," he told her. "Clean up and wash your hair while I'm gone. Check yourself good for any more cuts and scrapes. If you find any, use the peroxide. I'll finish your chin and a few other things when I get back."

"Better hurry," she said, drawing his hands around her rib cage inside her bra and closing his fingers over her breasts.

They were fuller than he'd thought and hot. She smiled at him, shyly in spite of her boldness, her gaze a vivid amber sheen in the steam clouding the room. Then she lowered her eyes to look at his hands on her breasts and made a soft little noise in her throat that undid him. Exploring the island could wait, he decided, exploring Hallie couldn't.

"Oh, Ellison." She threw her head back and tightened her grip on his wrists as he circled her nipples with his thumbs. "Oh God, please don't go."

"I have to," he said, just to tease her.

"Then I have to do this," she said, slipping her arms out of her bra straps and clamping them around his neck.

He had only a moment to spread his hands on the pebbled-glass shower door behind her before her right leg locked around his left knee and pulled him off balance. He stumbled against her, laughing, with only half his weight.

"Where the hell did you learn that?"

"In desperate, repressed virgin class."

"Oh, hell." Quade felt himself throb in the vee of her spread legs. "You said you weren't."

"I'm not. I've been to bed with a man. Once." Her lashes swept down, then lifted. "So technically—"

"How long ago?"

"What difference does that make?"

"A lot. How long?"

Her lashes swept down again and stayed down. "Four years."

"While you were in England, at Oxford."

"Yes," she mumbled. "In the back of a Mini."

"I'd love to know how you managed that. But not now," he added, when she raised her head and opened her mouth to tell him. "Tell me later." He pressed a kiss against her mouth. "Tell me after I show you what you missed in the back of that Mini."

He started with the salty hollow of her throat, swirling a slow circle there with his tongue until she moaned and her leg slipped down his calf. Then he slid his tongue down the middle of her torso, leaving a wet, shivery trail in the sand clinging between her breasts, walking his hands down the door until he was on his knees between her legs.

He raised his head to look at her as he undid the snap and zipper of her jeans. She was watching him, her face and her eyes luminous, steam glistening on her breasts. Quade thought about licking them dry but didn't, just hooked his thumbs inside the waistband of her jeans and her panties and tugged them past her hips. Much as he wanted to taste her, he didn't, just nuzzled her soft curls until she moaned.

Then he got to his feet, backed her into the door and hooked his fingers over the top. Her hands slid into his back pockets and pulled him hard against her. He closed his eyes, pressed his forehead against the glass, then rocked back and looked at her.

"Unzip me," he said.

She did with shaky fingers, fighting the snap and the brass pull. She managed it without catching him, eased the elastic band of his briefs over his bulge and touched one finger to the tip.

"Oh my." She raised just her eyes to his face, her lashes jeweled with damp, a breathy catch in her voice. "Is this mine all mine?"

"Yours all yours." Quade pressed his lips to the bridge of her nose and felt his throat ache.

He gave her a minute to explore, savoring the slow up and down rub of her curled finger, then eased her off the door and opened it. A gush of steam rolled out, dewing her skin deliciously. She stepped inside the stall and backed into the far corner while he shucked off his clothes.

When he followed her inside and shut the door, she gave a soft mewl and spread her palm on his chest. It was still plenty sore and plenty ugly, the bruise a vicious indigo swirl laced with broken blood vessels. He winced a bit when she touched her fingernail to the point of impact, a scabbed-over scratch above his left nipple.

She looked up at him, blinking. "The bullet did this?"

"Body armor keeps you from getting killed," he said, "not from getting hurt."

"Oh, Ellison." She kissed the bruise and laid her cheek against it, gently, her mouth and her fingertips raking lightly through his chest hair. "No wonder you didn't get up."

"Knocked me cold for about thirty seconds." He slipped an arm around her, his hand up her back to cradle her head.

Her neck was no bigger than his wrist. A neat little snap and she'd never know what hit her. A helluva thing to think about, standing in the shower with a lush, sweet little tough girl aching to have him inside her, but it helped keep his mind off his own ache. The one in his heart.

"What did you do?" She lifted her head and looked at him. "Lay low in the bushes and wait for Maxwell to bring the Admiral back?"

"Nope." Time to distract her, Quade decided, reversing their positions to stand her under the spray and wet her hair. "I went over the wall a few seconds behind you and ran like hell."

"With that?" Hallie raked her streaming hair out of her face and nodded, wide-eyed, at the bruise.

"No guts, no glory." She wrinkled her nose at him and he grinned, picked up the shampoo he'd stuck inside the stall and poured some into his left hand. "The Admiral's goons chased me all the way to Route 50. I hid in a ditch until Max came looking for me."

"But he *did* take the Admiral back to the compound?"

"Alive and kicking, just like I told you." Quade shifted them around again and rubbed his palms together. "And screaming, Max said."

"I can do that," Hallie told him, when he fingered the shampoo into her hair.

"But I want to." He captured the soap he'd put in the holder on the wall in one slippery hand and gave it to her. "Make yourself useful as well as decorative."

He scrubbed her hair while she soaped her palms and started making slow circles on his chest. Quade let himself relax and react. She loved it. Her breath caught and so did his, watching her face flush and her eyes round with pleasure when his muscles jumped beneath her touch.

"Oh golly, wow," she breathed, lifting her glistening, amber gaze to look at him. "You really do want me."

"Did you think I didn't? That I'm doing you a favor?"

"Yes, frankly." She held his gaze without blinking. "But I decided I didn't care."

Quade folded her into his arms, laid her cheek against his soapy chest and his chin against her shampoo-stiff hair. He closed his eyes and savored the wet, sleek feel of her and felt himself go weak in the knees. It had been six years since anything had made him feel like this, since he'd stood at attention at his court martial, heard his sentence read and watched his naval career go up in smoke.

"I want you more than I've ever wanted anyone in my life," he told her, and meant it. "Let me show you," he murmured, turning her again to rinse her hair.

She tipped her head back, clasped her arms about his waist and let him. The arch of her throat made the pulse in the hollow between her collarbones throb visibly. He kissed it and swung her around, slipped down on his knees and heard her moan, deep and low, either from the needle of the spray on her breasts or from the touch of his tongue. He didn't know or care, just cupped her against him and took her with his mouth.

She came apart on him almost instantly, her nails digging into his shoulders. She was still shuddering when she slid down his chest, her nails raking through his hair. He caught one nipple lightly in his teeth, slipped his fingers inside her and made her climax again. This time she screamed. When he finally let her stop, she slumped into his arms, limp and liquid, quivering and whimpering and trying to open her legs.

"No baby, not here." He cupped his hand over her and kissed her mouth, an open, wet kiss so she could taste how sweet she was. She moaned and he scooped her up in his arms. "Shut off the water."

She did, he kicked open the stall and carried her to the bed in the back bedroom. The French doors stood open, purple and indigo evening swirling in from the lanai. Hallie shivered and cuddled closer. Quade laid her down, stood to draw the mosquito net, then eased himself over her on his hands and knees. He intended just to warm her, but her legs were open. So were her eyes, wide and pleading.

"Please, Ellison, now," she whispered, winding her arms around his neck and pulling his mouth over hers.

Her tongue slid sweetly into his mouth as his fingers trailed unsteadily down the length of her. He felt a jolt when he touched her, molten and ready for him. He lifted his eyes to her face, but got distracted by her breasts and her taut little tummy quivering in anticipation.

His throat was so tight he couldn't speak. He rose on his knees, lifted her hands from his neck to his hips and managed to croak, "Keep 'em right there."

He eased into her, felt her arch to take him, clamped his hands on the rattan headboard behind her and hung on for dear life. *Oh God. So this was heaven.* And he was still alive. He felt his arms shudder and breathed deeply to get a grip on himself. When he did, Hallie arched again and he slid the rest of the way inside her.

"Oh, *Ellison.*"

She put about four extra *l*'s in his name, a throb in her voice that vibrated up his spine. She said it again and he pushed into her, withdrew and slowly entered again. He wanted to slam and bang himself into her but he didn't, just kept a hold on the headboard and stroked her, stoked her and himself, her nails gouging and goading him.

He wanted to spend the night inside her, the rest of his life hearing her say his name with those extra *l*'s. He thought he could manage the night at least, until she slipped her hand between them and touched him just above their joining. He said—no, he shouted something, maybe her name, and thrust into her hard, twice, three times, exploding and spilling and bellowing something else—heaven knew what—when she went into spasms around him. Not once, but twice.

She was still shuddering when he withdrew, rolled onto his back and took her with him. There were tears on his chest and on her face. He wiped them away, caught a corner of the sheet and covered her, cuddled her. She writhed against him, murmuring, until she fell asleep.

Wasn't life a bitch. Quade rested his chin against Hallie's temple and listened to her soft breathing. He was most likely going to die. If not tomorrow, the next day, and at last he'd found a multiorgasmic woman.

19

IT WAS A DISGUSTINGLY macho thing to think, but it kept Quade's mind off how much Hallie really meant to him. He got up to shave, brush his teeth and check the house and grounds. He didn't think Mai Lu would fool with bugs and she hadn't, but that didn't mean they weren't being watched.

Quade could almost feel eyes in the jungle beyond the garden. He stood on the lanai outside the bedroom smoking a cigarette, in cotton trousers and a long-sleeved shirt for protection against the mosquitoes. Mai Lu had left a can of repellent, but he'd had enough of stinking to high heaven. The deep drags he took flared the tip of the cigarette, still nothing but palm fronds moved in the liquid tropical night.

"That's right, pal, I'm watching you." Quade exhaled through his nose. "C'mon out and we'll play a little one-on-one."

He probably shouldn't have let Hallie dissuade him from scoping out the cay but you only lived—and died— once. One more sleepless night wasn't much. Especially since this one could be his last. And Hallie's.

For the first time in a long time Quade was scared. He'd been in worse cracks than this, squeezed tighter between a rock and a hard place, but never with someone who meant more to him than drawing his next breath.

He had no idea of the time but figured it was about eleven-thirty. His watch had bought it at six-twelve. He hadn't noticed the crystal he'd bashed to smithereens against the cruiser's hull until he'd turned on the bathroom light, the door half-shut so he wouldn't waken Hallie.

Was it Nino or Sebu out there? Or one of the flunkies he'd seen loading the freighter? Once the tide receded, dropping a watchman on the west end of the cay would have been easy.

He heard sheets rustle and Hallie groan, flipped his cigarette off the lanai and went inside. As exhausted as she was, he'd expected her to sleep all night. He could just see her through the mosquito net draped like a milky shadow around the bed, pushed up on her elbows, her head in her hands.

"Hey, tough girl." He slipped through the net and sat on the edge of the mattress. "Bad dream?"

"My life is a bad dream." She flopped on her stomach and flung out her arms, grouchy and still half-asleep. "I'm hungry. Will you make me something to eat?"

"Sure. What d'you want?"

"Surprise me." She shoved up on her elbow and blinked at him sleepily, her backbone a pale gleam in the near darkness. "I can't cook, y'know. Not a lick."

"Yes, you can." He caught her arm and gave her a yank that landed her, laughing, half twisted in the sheet in his lap and in his arms. "Right here where it counts."

She made a languid noise and wound her arms around him. "Doesn't this fade after a while once the fuse burns down a little?"

"Not if you do it right." Quade lifted her, kissed her and felt her melt when he murmured against her mouth, "And you, my sweet, do it very, *very* right."

"I love you, Ellison," she said softly, twisting his heart in his chest.

He kissed her again, then gave her a sound smack on the fanny. "Get up." He snagged the robe he'd found in the closet from the foot of the bed where he'd tossed it earlier. "Before I get hungry."

Quade shut the French doors, went into the kitchen and flipped on the lights, startled a gecko that skittered away into a corner. Close one, he thought, listening to water run and the toilet flush. Lucky for him close only counted in horseshoes and hand grenades.

By the time Hallie appeared, he'd lit a fistful of fat candles provided as backup for the generator-powered lights that had already dimmed twice. He was humming "Are You Lonesome Tonight?" when she stopped barefoot in the bedroom doorway in a strapless tropical-print sarong.

"Is that the only song you know?" she asked.

"Why, no, ma'am." Quade forked a lock of hair over his forehead, twitched his upper lip at her twice and dropped his voice into a lower register. "What would y'all like t'hear?"

He flung out his arms, turned his head to the right, twitched his wrist, looked back at Hallie and twitched his lip again. She blinked at him, stunned.

When he started singing "Blue Suede Shoes," her lips parted in amazement. When he rolled his pelvis at her, she flushed to the roots of her hair. When he changed the chorus to blue suede boots, she slapped a hand against the wall and shrieked with laughter.

It was all the encouragement he needed to swivel-hip his way across the room and scoop her against him. Tango-style, he boogied her to the table and a chair.

"Help." Hallie wiped tears from her eyes. "I'm stranded on Shark Island with an Elvis impersonator."

"Thank you." He pronounced it "Thaunk yoooou" and twitched his lip one last time. "Thank you ver-ra much."

She laughed, her face flushed and glowing, her crinkled, crush-dried hair picking up the gleam of the candles. Quade dropped a kiss on the top of her head and sat down across the table from her. "Want to eat here or in bed?"

She swept her lashes down shyly. "This is fine."

The candle flames, stirred by the ceiling fans he turned on, flickered in her eyes. A bar of pale shadow sliced the base of her throat and sent a prickle of dread across the back of his neck.

"High protein, low fat and minimal cholesterol." Hallie speared a hunk of cheese with her fork, a slice of cold ham and orange wedges off a platter onto her plate. "Mai Lu wasn't kidding when she said she wants me in good shape."

"Mai Lu never kids. Fanatics have no sense of humor."

She picked up a glass of ice water. "Bottled, I trust?"

"Nothing but." Quade lifted his glass, clinked it against hers and smiled. "To us."

"To us." She drank and put the glass down almost empty.

Quade got up to refill it, left the pitcher he'd put in the fridge on the table. Hallie had eaten everything but the oranges and refilled her plate.

"You don't like oranges," he said.

"Not especially."

"Want a mango?"

"No, thanks." She drank and gazed at him over the candle burning in a saucer beside the pitcher. "If you've got any ideas about getting us out of here, I'd like to hear them."

"Our best bet is to jump Nino for the boat, unless I come up with a better plan once I've given this mosquito-infested lump the once-over."

"What if Sebu comes with him? Or Conan? And don't—" Hallie flung up a warning hand "—say it."

"I won't." Quade smiled and folded his arms. "If Mai Lu lent you a bikini you can be the diversion."

"*Me?*" She splayed her fingers on her breast. "In a bikini a good laugh, maybe, but not much of a diversion."

"I'd say buck naked, but I'm the jealous type."

She laughed, leaned an elbow beside her plate, her chin on her hand, and smiled. "I love you, tough guy."

He leaned across the table and kissed her mouth. "I want a mango. You?"

"No, thanks." Her smile faded. "I'm full."

With a table knife so dull it wouldn't cut butter, Quade did his best to peel and slice one. He hadn't found a single thing so far that could double as a weapon. The meat and cheese had been precut, the dishes, pitcher and glasses were plastic. Hallie's robe didn't even have a belt. His belt had been confiscated on the seaplane.

He washed the mango and popped a piece into his mouth on his way back to the table. Hallie pushed her chair sideways, tucked one leg beneath her and folded her arms.

"You can't say it, can you?"

"Say what?"

"You can't say you love me."

The mango stuck in his throat. God he wanted to say it, but he couldn't. She didn't love him, anyway; she only thought she did. After the hell she'd been through the last ten days it wouldn't surprise him if she thought the world was flat, but give her a good night's sleep once they were out of this, a couple days of nobody stalking her or threatening to slit her throat and she'd see him for what he was, wonder what the hell she'd ever seen in him.

Quade knew what he saw in Hallie. His birthright, the fairy tale his life had once been. She was the embodiment of everything he'd believed in until the Admiral had taught him you can't believe in anything. She'd made the fairy tale real again and made him wish to God he was an enchanted prince. The part of him that always had and he supposed always would yearn for Camelot would always love Hallie. Even when reality kicked her in the head and she could no longer stand the sight of him.

"I didn't think I had to say it," he told her with his best bedroom smile. "I thought I'd proved it."

"You've proved that you're a very crafty liar, Ellison H. Quade III. You know as well as I do that short of the Marines storming the beach there's no way off this stinking island, yet you light candles and give me that hokey 'To us' toast. You even say you want to marry me. Why stop short of saying you love me? Afraid we *might* get out of here and I'll hold you to it?"

"Maybe I'm afraid you won't hold me to it."

"Oh *please*." She rolled her eyes. "Not that I'm a monster crap again."

"You know I am. You said so yourself. You were scared to death of me in L.A. and you had every right to be."

"I hear what you tell me but I *know* what I see. You gave me your money clip and you smashed a three-thousand-dollar watch distracting that shark. A monster wouldn't have."

Could be worse. She could have kept her eyes open a moment longer and seen Nino and Sebu wrestle him to the deck when he'd tried to jump the rail and swim to her rescue. Not one of his finest moments. He was glad she'd missed it.

"This isn't your world, Hallie, it's mine. I'm used to the pressure and the stress. You're not. You need me to hang on to like you needed my money clip. I'm flattered, believe me, but once you get back to the real world—"

"Don't you *dare* say it!" She shot out of her chair so suddenly she almost fell. Quade was on his feet and around the table to catch her, but she recovered her balance and skittered away from him like the gecko. "Don't you *dare* tell me I don't know my own feelings! I am *not* suffering some stress-induced delusion! I *love* you and don't you *dare* try to tell me I *don't!*"

She whirled into the bedroom, slamming the door so hard she startled the gecko out of its corner. It scuttled out the partly-open door. Quade followed, lit a cigarette and stood in the dark wondering where the Admiral and Max were and wishing to God they'd hurry. Then he went inside and put the food away, washed the dishes and listened at Hallie's door. Nothing. Not even tears.

He made instant coffee, drank two cups, smoked another cigarette, took a shower to ease the fatigue knotting his back and shoulder muscles, washed out his jeans and Hallie's in the bathtub and draped them over the lanai rail. Mai Lu had left him a pair but they were a lousy fit.

He took naps standing against a wall like he'd stood against bulkheads on midnight watches. An hour before dawn his jeans were as dry as they were going to get. He put them on along with his sweater.

Unless he was dispensable, the watchman would be picked up before the tide. Hallie would be safe enough for the few minutes it would take him to jog down the beach and check. Quade slipped out the front door and reached the western tip of the cay just as a slight figure darted out of the palm fringe and waded out to meet a small motor boat. Sebu helped the man over the side. Nino was at the wheel.

Too early for the morning check, Quade thought, watching the boat churn away at half throttle toward the big island. He made sure it didn't double back, then slipped into the trees to make sure the watchman had been alone.

Cautiously he made his way through the jungle around the back of the house, aiming toward the vantage point he'd selected from the lanai and found a beaten-down patch of undergrowth. He also found the high-powered, infrared binoculars the watchman had left behind.

"I love inept help," Quade murmured, smiling as he picked them up and stepped out into the garden.

Hallie was on the lanai, setting things on the table. She had on khaki shorts and a short-sleeved, unbuttoned jungle-print shirt over a strapless blue bikini top. His mouth went dry at the swell of her breasts, drier still when he stepped onto the lanai and she looked at him. Her amber eyes were as flat and unblinking as the geckos.

"Where'd you find those?" she asked.

"In the brush. Our night watchman left them."

She nodded and said, "I'm sure you already looked, but this is all the stuff I could find that I thought might be useful."

Quade had, but was impressed with her collection. A table knife, a hard plastic dinner plate, a stack of three towels and one she'd torn into strips and tied into a rope. He picked it up, examined her midshipman-perfect square knots and lifted his eyes to her face.

"With my teeth," she said, answering the question he hadn't asked. "You're probably strong enough to break the plate. I'm not, I tried. It might shatter into some nice sharp shards. I think the knife is useless, but you might have muscle enough to—"

She broke off and bit her lip. Quade picked up the last item on the table, her mother's pearls. "What's this?" he asked, though he already knew.

"A garotte."

"Won't work. String's too weak."

"No, it isn't. I restrung it on two-hundred-pound-test fishing line."

"You *what?*" A cold jolt shot up Quade's back. Two hundred was strong enough to land a marlin. Or Nino or Sebu. Maybe even Conan, if he took him off guard.

"I snuck it out of the safe in the library. I had the combination for a while until the Admiral found out and changed it." She glanced away from him and bit her lip. "For a while there, I was nearly as paranoid as he is."

And she'd gotten it past Conan. *God, what a woman.* Quade smiled and slipped the pearls into his pocket.

"You want to hang around for Nino to take attendance?"

"No." She looked at him. "I want to go with you."

"Okay. Let's grab some chow—"

"Done." Hallie lifted the black nylon bag from a chair. "Four bottles of mineral water and nothing that will spoil. I know that much about food preparation."

Plus she'd found time to French-braid her hair.

20

FROM A TINY BAMBOO clearing about an eighth of a mile away and halfway up a hillside, Hallie watched the cruiser bump up to the dock and Nino slog up the beach into the house. A moment later he came out and waved at Sebu.

"He's smiling, the son of a bitch," Quade muttered, passing her the binoculars.

Actually he was grinning, Hallie saw, as Nino's broad face leaped into close view. When Sebu started up the beach, a third man came out of the wheelhouse with an Uzi.

"Sharkskin jacket from L.A.?" Quade asked.

"Yes," Hallie said. *Harbinger of doom*, she thought. Wherever Sharkskin went, trouble followed.

"Well, well." Quade bent his elbow on his knee and rubbed his chin. "Mai Lu has pulled in her point man."

"Does that mean what I think it means?"

"Yep. She doesn't need his eyes and ears out there anymore. She needs him here."

"So the Admiral's on his way?"

"I'd say so. Sharkskin didn't come home for Christmas."

"But how could the Admiral get here so fast?"

"He said he knew about Conan. That means he knew about Mai Lu, too. Or suspected."

Turning the binoculars toward the house, Hallie saw Nino and Sebu walk around it toward the lanai. They were laughing, loud enough for Hallie to hear. "What's so funny?"

"Beats me. Maybe they think we went swimming."

Or hope, Hallie thought, handing Quade the glasses.

"What the hell," he muttered, as Sebu removed a section of latticework covering the crawlspace under the lanai and Nino dropped to the grass on his back and scrunched his head and shoulders under it.

Sebu squatted at his feet and watched, much as Hallie did beside Quade. When Nino got stuck in the narrow space, Sebu grasped his ankles and pulled him out. It should've been funny but it wasn't.

"Don't they realize we could be watching them?"

"I don't think they care, babe."

The endearment sounded absent and offhand, gave Hallie a quiver and almost made her forget she was angry with Quade. For the things he'd said to her, for treating her like a simple-minded twit, for respecting and not infringing on her right to be angry.

He'd only touched her twice on their hike up the hill, taking her hand to help her over rough spots. Miffed as she was, Hallie ached to have him touch her again. Like he had in the shower, right here, right now, with bugs everywhere and whispers in the grass that made her nerves jump.

But he watched Nino and Sebu lumber back to the cruiser. When they climbed aboard he stood and trained the binoculars on Sharkskin as he stepped into the wheelhouse.

"Just the three of them." He lowered the glasses as the cruiser backed out into the bay and swung around toward the big island. "C'mon. Let's see what's under there."

Hallie took Quade's left hand and pulled herself up. The cruiser had vanished by the time they reached the lanai. Quade removed the panel, went down on his back, caught the edge and swung himself under. He stayed under long enough for Hallie's heart to start pounding.

"What is it?" she asked, when he came back out.

"The biggest, nastiest, most wickedly-wired bomb I've ever seen." Quade clenched his jaw and brushed cobwebs off the yellow-and-green tropical-print shirt he'd traded his sweater for. "Somebody around here is a goddamn genius."

"Conan." Hallie thought instantly of the pagoda pin, a moment later of the embassy satchel, and felt the blood drain from her face. "Mai Lu's going to blow us to kingdom come, just like Rico."

"*Exactly* like Rico." There was an edge in Quade's voice Hallie had never heard before. "I should've strangled her when she damn near killed Max."

"How many more bombs do you suppose there are?"

"I don't know." Quade lifted his sunglasses by the earpiece, folded them into his shirt pocket and started around the house. "But I'm gonna find out."

"When and why," Hallie asked, hurrying to keep up with him, "did Mai Lu almost kill Maxwell?"

"About seven years ago in Manila, damn near gutted him with a beer bottle. She thought we were Shore Patrol come to shake down the dive where she turned tricks when she wasn't with the Admiral or helping Rico wire car bombs."

There it is, Hallie thought. *Payment in kind.* A chill shot across the nape of her neck.

"She never did figure out the Admiral was feeding her bogus intelligence," Quade said, kicking sand behind him as he strode across the beach. "But somebody did, 'cause somebody set us up."

"The Admiral?" Hallie was almost running to keep up.

"He swore he told Mai Lu we were going to make that particular drop for him." Quade stopped and eyed the dock critically. "She said he didn't, that she was tipped that the Shore Patrol was rousting all the dockside hookers to take V.D. tests."

"She almost killed Maxwell to avoid a blood test?"

"Not the needle. The rap sheet and fingerprints. In Mai Lu's line of work, you need a low profile."

"I take it this happened before the embassy satchel?"

"About six months, yeah. Max was still in the hospital when I was court-martialed."

So he hadn't been around to help Quade like he had in Middleburg. "Does Maxwell think the Admiral set you up?"

"I never asked." Quade went out on the deck, dropped to his stomach, gripped the edge and looked underneath. Then he came back to Hallie looking like he wanted to strangle somebody. "Just a second. I need to hit something."

He selected a palm tree and gave it three savage backkicks. Then he turned around, nudged his cigarettes out of his shirt pocket and lit one.

"There's enough dynamite under the deck to blow up New Jersey. Mai Lu expects the Admiral to come ashore here to get you." He uttered a nasty word beginning with *f* and dragged on his cigarette. "I should've found this crap yesterday."

Remembering the shower in vivid, blood-pumping detail, Hallie flushed and looked at her scratched shins. She started when Quade raised her chin on his bent index finger.

"I'm not sorry and don't you be, either," he said gently. "I just don't like surprises."

"I'll bet there are charges all over this cay."

"I'll bet you're right. And I know just where to look." Quade lifted his gaze to the top of the hill they'd climbed partway. "Get the rest of the water and anything edible that won't rot and let's get the hell out of here."

While he retrieved the black nylon bag, Hallie went inside and changed into her jeans. They'd be hot, but her shins itched like fire. When she came out of the bedroom, Quade was carrying a wicker settee toward the door. "What are you doing?"

He stopped and looked back at her. "Writing our ticket outta here, I hope," he said, turning the settee sideways through the door. When he came back, Hallie asked, "Are we building a raft?"

"A bonfire. I can't defuse that mother under the lanai. I've never seen anything like it." Quade tossed the fanback chair out the door. "I'd say Mai Lu expects the Admiral to come in hard and fast just about dark or a little after."

"With what?" Hallie asked, stuffing oranges into the bag.

"His own private little navy." Quade grabbed a table and pitched it outside. "I suspected he had one, and your mother told Arnie he did twenty-three years ago."

"He said he'd come after you himself." Hallie put the peroxide and Merthiolate in the bag and looked at Quade. "And you told me that was the rest of the plan. What plan?"

"To lure the Admiral to Honolulu." He tossed another table out the door and lit a cigarette. "You were supposed to ship out with Arnie, and Max was supposed to drop enough hints while he drove him around so he'd know where to come. Max and I planned to wait for him and Conan to show and make sure that for once Hiram Whitcomb cleaned up his own mess."

"Except somebody told Mai Lu." Hallie put two packs of cigarettes in the bag. "You know who it was, don't you?"

"Not really." Parking his cigarette in the corner of his mouth, Quade dropped to his heels and rolled up a rattan mat. "Haven't had much time to think about it."

"C'mon, tough guy. Everything points straight to him."

Quade threw her a sharp, upward glance. "Okay, Rhodes scholar. Who?"

"Maxwell. Maybe he thinks the Admiral set him up or maybe he thinks the Admiral put Mai Lu up to killing him, but either way, he has a helluva motive to see both of them dead. What better way than to pit them against each other?"

"Maybe." Something flickered in Quade's eyes as he scooped up the mat and lugged it outside.

Hallie followed, picked up a table and carried it toward the palm trees on the edge of the jungle about sixty yards from the house. Unless the wind switched, it would fan the fire away from the bomb toward the west end of the cay. She put the table down, sat on it and watched Quade slam the fanback chair against a palm trunk hard enough to break it, then stack the pieces at the base of the tree.

"Let me guess," she said. "If Mai Lu means to keep me alive to cut my throat for the Admiral, she'll send the cruiser."

"With any luck."

"What if Conan's aboard with an Uzi instead?"

"Calculated risk." Quade rose and took off his shirt. "At 2000 we're dead. Possibly earlier if the Admiral shows on schedule. She's got something to keep him pinned here until the charges blow, and I don't intend to get caught in a firefight. Not without an Uzi of my own."

He went back to smashing chairs, sweat sheening on his arms and his chest. Hallie felt her pulse pound watching him, remembering how his muscles had quivered at her touch.

"So when do we start toasting marshmallows?"

"'Bout an hour or so before sunset." He stopped and wiped his tattoo across his forehead. "That gives us plenty of time to climb that hill and see if we can see what Mai Lu's got planned for us and the Admiral."

Hallie got up, stripped to her bikini and started lugging furniture across the sand. Every few minutes she had to stop and hike up the strapless top that kept trying to slip off her breasts. It took them about an hour to break up the furniture and stack the bonfire in a strip about twenty yards long, a yard high and a foot or so deep at the edge of the jungle. When they'd finished, Quade picked up his shirt and rubbed his chest.

"Do you want to stay mad?" he asked. "Or make love in the shower before we head out of here?"

Hallie wanted things she'd never dreamed of before and looked like she'd never have unless the bonfire worked. They flashed through her head in a heartbeat, made a lump in her throat, and they all centered on Ellison Quade.

"I want to get the hell off this island," she told him.

"So do I." He cupped her face and bent his head to kiss her. "But I want to make love to you one more time."

He didn't say in case it was the last time, but he didn't have to. Hallie scooped up her clothes and led him into the house. He followed with a quirky smile on his face, undressed while she started the shower, then peeled her out of the bikini.

Hallie drew him under the spray and washed him. He stood still watching her, smiling at the trembling of her fingertips. Then he took the soap and caressed her with it while he kissed her and murmured things that made her knees go weak. When he picked her up she opened her legs and wrapped them around him, locked her arms around his neck as he pressed her to the wall and slipped inside her.

"Oh God, Hallie." He leaned his forehead against hers and cupped her tight against him. "If Mai Lu doesn't send the cruiser I want to die like this."

"You got it, tough guy." Hallie blinked back tears and terror to smile at him. "But not until you're very old and too weak to hold me up."

"I'll never be that old," he said, and surged into her.

Hallie clung to him, praying to every god she could think of, in all eight languages she knew, that she'd live to be loved like this every day for the rest of her life. She tried to arch against the wall to meet him, straining to give him as much of herself as she could.

"Oh God, baby." Quade went still and trembling inside her. "Don't do that. Not yet."

"Don't do what?" Hallie asked breathlessly.

"Tighten up like that. I'll tell you when." He lifted his head and looked at her, his eyes almost black with desire like they'd been in the dream she'd had aboard *Halimedes*. "You must've been first in your class."

"Second, actually."

"I meant your repressed, desperate virgin class."

Hallie laughed, Quade groaned and pushed into her, quick and deep, then lifted his hands from her bottom and spread them against the tiled wall. "Tell me you're ready." His voice was rough-edged and raw. "God please tell me."

"Always," Hallie murmured against his mouth.

"Hold on to me."

She wrapped her arms around his neck and hung on. With a growl Hallie felt at the back of her throat, Quade thrust into her. She closed her eyes and tipped her head back. He nipped at her throat, at one nipple and then the other, the rake of his teeth fanning flames to each breast sucked tight in his mouth. She cried his name, clutching handfuls of his wet hair, and held him as he thrust into her one last time.

For this time, anyway. Clinging to him fiercely, Hallie stroked his hair and smiled as he lifted his head.

"I love it when you say my name with all those extra *l*'s," he told her, nibbling her bottom lip.

She said it again, rolling the *l* on the back of her tongue, watched him smile and his eyes turn a deep, smoky gray. No more tundra, not anymore. Not ever again.

"Say it again," he said thickly.

Hallie did, felt heat rise when his lashes swept down over his eyes and he stirred inside her. "Oh, Ellison." She curved her hand around his jaw, her voice trembling. "Could we—I mean—can you—" She knew the words but couldn't say them.

"Turn off the water," Quade finished.

He carried her to bed and took her on top of him, fondling and kissing and biting and suckling her until she could no longer draw a steady breath. Then he touched a spot that sent her soaring and moaning, raking at his shoulders until she sighed and almost sobbed and collapsed on his chest. He wrapped his arms around her and kissed her hair.

"We ought to burn this mattress," he said. "Or have it bronzed."

21

THEY DECIDED TO BURN IT, along with the sheets, pillows, mosquito nets and the mattress from the other bed. Castoff like everything else, the ticking was worn and thin with small tears that split easily in Quade's strong hands. They tucked the batting and linens around the broken furniture in fist-size wads, then stepped back and admired the bonfire.

"It'll go up like a match," Quade said, satisfied.

"What about the jungle? Isn't it too wet to burn?"

"It'll smoke like crazy if nothing else, and that ought to get Mai Lu's attention." Quade took Hallie's hand, the binoculars and the bag and they started up the hill into the jungle.

It was a wretched climb and nearly midday by the angle of the sun when Hallie stumbled out of the trees behind him, her ankle throbbing, onto the bank of the rock-choked stream that formed the cataract. Niagara Falls it wasn't, slipping almost silently over the rim of the cay.

"If I intended to blow this place to hell," Quade said, bending on one knee beside the stream to scoop up a handful of water, "I'd set my charge up there."

He nodded at a smaller cascade with a fifteen-or-so-foot fall about as many yards to their left, lifted his cupped hand to his mouth, tasted and then drank. He swung the bag off his shoulder, scarcely breathing hard.

"I suppose you're gonna go look," Hallie said, letting her shuddering knees fold her onto the ground beside him.

"Yep," he replied, sprang up and went.

Hallie sprawled on the bank. To hell with the bugs and snakes. They could eat her alive. She closed her eyes until the whisk of Quade's hurried footsteps opened them.

"You gotta see this." He pulled the binoculars out of the bag with one hand and caught her wrist with the other.

"No, I don't," Hallie said tiredly.

"Yes, you do," he said, and yanked her to her feet.

Quade had to tow her up the gentle but rock-jumbled slope leading to the top of the little falls. The view was staggering and so was Hallie when he handed her the field glasses and pointed her toward the sprawl of the big island.

"Holy moley." Gooseflesh shot down her arms as she scanned a harbor on the northwestern coast and counted fourteen gunboats. "You said the military avoids these islands."

"You see any numbers, any flags? Those are mercs, pirates for hire and Mai Lu's left-wing pals."

"Lions and tigers and bears, oh, my. A regular armada."

"Close but no cigar. Mai Lu's expecting trouble, all right. Very big and very soon."

"You don't suppose the Admiral raised the fleet?"

"Don't I wish," Quade said feelingly. "He'd have to go to the Pentagon but he can't. This is private. He's got his own little fighting force, don't you worry."

He took the binoculars from her and made a three-sixty sweep of the bay and the ocean beyond. Hallie sensed his intensity, the excitement building in him and in herself.

"Look behind that rock about two yards from your left foot," he said. "Don't touch, not even the rock."

Hallie didn't want to but she did and felt her mouth turn to sand. Several sticks of dynamite were wired to a timer tucked into the grass sprouting around the rock.

"Set for eight o'clock and you can't defuse it, right?"

"Yes and no," Quade replied.

"Who the hell *is* Conan?"

"Max ran him through every contact he has. Interpol has a photo about ten years old that *could* be him. No name or history. Just a description and his M.O.—explosives." Quade lowered the glasses and lit a cigarette. "If I were the Admiral I'd hang off the horizon as long as I could, then strike at sunset with everything I have."

"Which is what, d'you suppose?"

"Beats me. Maybe we'll get lucky and get a peek before we have to go light our fire." He grinned at Hallie.

"Or flick our Bic," she said, wagging her eyebrows.

They laughed. Gallows humor, but it helped.

They spent the afternoon watching a couple of fishing boats and a small freighter meander in and out of the bay. Hallie wasn't hungry but Quade made her eat. They drank from the stream, then he took off his shirt, spread it in a shady spot and led her to it.

She dipped her hand in his pocket, withdrew her mother's pearls and put them on. He smiled watching her. Hallie was a raw recruit at this, but she was pretty sure she'd seen the first hint of a thaw in his eyes at the Admiral's party. She saw it again once she'd fastened the clasp.

"So sweet and so sexy." Quade traced the pearls with the index finger of his left hand while he unbuttoned her blouse with his right. "I love it."

How about me? Hallie wanted to ask, but didn't. Instead, she put her arms around him and kissed him. He made love to her slowly and mostly with his mouth because she was tender.

"I can't believe we're doing this," she said, clinging to him shakily. "I can't believe I even want to."

"You're tense as a bowstring and so am I," he murmured. "It'll relax you, believe me."

And it did until midafternoon. They'd climbed to the top of the little falls and Hallie was yawning when Quade sprang up and swung the binoculars seaward.

"What is it?" she asked, scrambling to her feet.

"Reflection," he said, moving the glasses slowly to the southeast. "Atta boy, Hiram. C'mon in like the sneaky old bastard you are. Show Mai Lu how you got to be an admiral."

And then Hallie saw it. A flicker on the far horizon, a little wink of light that had no reason to be there—unless it was a ship changing course, the sun reflecting off its hull or maybe its tower as it made the correction.

"That was a quick turn. What d'you think? Ten knots?"

"Ten, easy." Quade lowered the glasses and smiled. "Very good, Rhodes scholar."

"I *am* the granddaughter of an admiral."

"Don't remind me." He shuddered and swept the binoculars north. "It gives me the creeps when I think his blood will run in the baby we might have made."

Hallie felt a jolt, took a quick, downward glance at her fingers clutching the fly of her jeans. She was blushing, Quade smiling when she lifted just her eyes to his face.

"I couldn't be. Could I?"

"Doubtful, but a man can dream." He gave her a quick kiss. "Then you'd have to marry me."

"Just try to get out of it, tough guy." Hallie snatched the glasses from him and saw another flicker of light to the north. "He's flanking the island."

"He'll hit the harbor and land a small force there." Quade pointed northeast, toward the wrist of the big island. "Both diversions to cover his main strike. He'll come straight down the pipe." His arm moved toward the mouth of the bay. "He'll send an amphib for you, probably, and deploy his big stuff—probably a light cruiser—to pound the hell out of Mai Lu. Nice cover to get you out."

"To get *us* out. The gunboats are weighing anchor."

"Lemme see." Quade took the glasses and looked.

Hallie watched him track the boats out of the harbor. They sailed around the island in two groups, the ten that went north coming first around the headland and making for open water.

"Shit." Quade gave her the binoculars and lit a cigarette with a quick spin of the wheel on his lighter and an angry snap of the lid against his palm. "Mai Lu's made him."

"But how?"

"Gotta be radar."

"Wouldn't we be able to see a dish from up here?"

"If there was one. It's probably on an outlying island." He dragged on his cigarette, then pointed toward a ribbon of smoke on the horizon. "And Old Iron Butt just found it."

"He likes surprises even less than you do."

"Don't I know it." Quade raised the glasses as the ships coming from the south appeared, two making for the mouth of the bay, the rest heading swiftly southeast.

It seemed to Hallie that no more than a few minutes passed, but when she looked inland to rest her eyes from the glare she saw the sun had slipped a notch lower. To the west the sky was beginning to swirl toward sunset.

"This doesn't bode well for us, does it?"

"No. I think it's time to get the hell off this powder keg." Quade took a drag from his cigarette and threw it in the stream, stuffed the binoculars into the bag and picked it up, took her hand and pulled her down the slope.

"What if Mai Lu doesn't send the cruiser?"

"Then we wait for the Admiral."

"What if he doesn't make it on time? Or what if Mai Lu just means to blow us up and not him?"

"Then we die at twenty hundred hours." Quade caught her against him in one arm as they slid to the bottom of the slope. "Naked on the beach making love to each other."

"Over my dead body," the Admiral said behind them.

Taking Hallie with him, Quade spun around to face him. The Admiral stood near the lip of the cataract, with John behind him and Phillip coiling a rope tied to a grappling hook.

Oh God, the cliff, Hallie thought. It had never crossed their minds to check it. Not once.

"One of those fishing boats," Quade whispered in her ear, "wasn't a fishing boat."

"Come here, Joanna," the Admiral said.

Hallie's hand flashed to her throat. The pearls, the damn pearls. "I'm not Joanna. I'm Hallie."

Her grandfather blinked at her, then tipped his head warily. He was dressed in jungle fatigues. So were John and Phillip, with slashes of green camouflage paint on their faces and pistols and knives belted to their waists.

"He's brainwashed you, hasn't he? That's why you can't remember your name."

"I remember it just fine. It's *Hallie*." From the corner of her eye she watched John circle behind them, felt Quade's eyes tracking him, too. "I'm your granddaughter."

The Admiral's gaze shifted to Quade and he reached for his sidearm. "I'll kill you for this, you son of a bitch."

"If you do I'll never speak to you again." Hallie flattened herself against Quade and felt his hands, steady as ever, cup her shoulders.

"Get out of the way, Joanna." The Admiral made an impatient wave with his pistol. "I have to do this. He won't go away. He keeps coming back and taking you, and you're the only thing I have of any value in this world."

Oh my God, Hallie thought. *Now he thinks Quade is Arnie. Is this a paranoid delusion, or is he sick?* He didn't look ill. He looked strong and tough and determined.

"I'm not a *thing*," she said. "I'm a person. That's where you keep dropping the ball, Granddad."

Hallie hadn't called him that in ten years, but did so now, torn between panic and pity, hoping she could get through to him. The Admiral's pistol wavered. Not with indecision, but to signal Phillip to move her out of the way.

"Please, Granddad, don't do this. For me, *please*."

The Admiral ignored her. Phillip kept coming. John was nowhere in sight. The jungle with its protective tangle of vegetation was no more than five yards away.

If the Admiral was thinking clearly enough, he wouldn't risk a shot that might draw attention from the big island.

If she timed it just right. Hallie waited until Phillip reached for her, then launched herself at him like a stone from a slingshot. Quade gave her a push and took a rolling dive into the undergrowth.

The Admiral didn't fire. Hallie thanked God and let Phillip drag her up to her grandfather. He slapped her.

"Strumpet." He shoved his pistol into its holster and nodded at Phillip. "Find him and kill him. Quietly."

"I don't think we need to bother with him, sir," John said, coming toward them along the bank. "There's enough dynamite at the top of the falls to blow this whole side of the island. The timer's set for twenty-hundred."

"Vengeful bitch." The Admiral's eyes narrowed as he glanced at his watch. It was, Hallie saw, nearly five forty-five. "Very well. Move out. Take the point, John."

"Aye, sir." He didn't salute, just melted into the trees ahead of them to the right.

Phillip took her elbow and pushed her along behind the Admiral. They were headed toward the western tip of the cay.

"Mai Lu checks on me twice a day," Hallie said to the Admiral's back. "I was absent this morning. If I'm absent tonight she may come looking for me."

"She'll be dead by then," he replied flatly.

He said no more to her, not even when they reached the beach and a small palm clearing fringing the sand where Sousa waited with a field radio and six other men with rifles. Phillip sat her down hard and moved off with the Admiral.

The radio squawked now and then but Hallie couldn't make out the scratchy, static-riddled voices. She wondered where Quade was, and John, and whether Nino and Sebu and Sharkskin would come this way with the cruiser when they found the lights on but nobody home.

The sun sank lower until twilight deepened the gloom beneath the palms and streaked the sand with purple and gold. The Admiral began to pace. Phillip lit a cigarette. The radio had been silent for a good ten minutes when it came suddenly to life in a burst of static that sounded like a thunderclap in the middle of a rainstorm.

"Admiral." Sousa turned toward him, the headset pressed to one ear. "Our pickup boat has been hit, sir."

Fear raced up Hallie's back and prickled across the nape of her neck. The Admiral spun on one heel, his hands folded behind his back. "How bad?"

Another crackle of thunder leaped from the radio and then there was nothing, not even static. Sousa blinked, stunned, at the Admiral.

"Get me the *Joanna*," he ordered briskly.

Get me the hell out of here. Hallie swallowed a lump of panic in her throat, drew a deep breath and smelled smoke.

Sousa tuned the radio to another frequency and handed the headset to the Admiral. Hallie listened to him talk to the commander of the *Joanna*, the light cruiser Quade said he had, she figured.

"Twenty minutes, gentlemen," the Admiral announced, turning away from the radio.

"Sir. Something's burning." Phillip pitched his cigarette away and rushed out of the trees.

The Admiral strode after him. No one stopped Hallie when she followed. Above the hillside a thick column of smoke drifted north toward the big island.

"What *idiot* torched the jungle!" the Admiral shouted.

The idiot I love, Hallie thought, though she had no idea why Quade had lit the bonfire.

The air crackled and snapped, the bamboo behind the palms shivered and John tumbled out of it, face first and unmoving on the sand. A second too late, Phillip and Sousa reached for their pistols.

"Don't gimme a reason," Quade said, stepping out of the trees with dirt and sweat streaking his face, the Uzi in his hands leveled at the Admiral's chest. "You can keep your sidearms, boys, so long as you aren't stupid."

"At ease," the Admiral said, and the two relaxed. "Nice of you to join us, Quade. It appears we'll be here a bit longer than I thought. We may need an extra hand."

It's a delusion, Hallie thought, hearing the calm rationality in his voice. *He slips in and out of reality.*

"You don't need a hand, Admiral, you need a platoon of marines," Quade told him. "There's a dozen gunboats blocking the mouth of the bay. Your cruiser'll get through but not in twenty minutes, and Mai Lu will be here in less than five. She's on her way with a couple dozen heavily-armed troops. Several looked very familiar, if you get my drift."

"Impossible." A finger of smoke snaked through the trees toward the Admiral. "I destroyed her organization."

"You missed a few." Quade batted a drift of burning ash out of his face with one hand. "If I were you I wouldn't make it easy for her. I'd get off this beach pronto."

The Admiral squared his shoulders. "The hell I will."

"Granddad, please." Hallie swept her hair, fanned by the wind feeding the fire, out of her eyes and wheeled toward him. "We're outnumbered 2.6 to 1."

"Hallie." The Admiral blinked at her, startled. "How did you get here? Where's your mother? Why are you wearing her necklace?"

"You gave it to me," she replied, shooting a panicked, help me look at Quade.

He shook his head, not stubbornly but hopelessly, even a bit sadly. A burst of automatic fire somewhere off to the left ripped through the dull roar of the burning jungle. Bits of debris were flaming on the sand, sizzling and hissing in the tide flooding up the beach.

The Admiral gripped Hallie's elbows and looked at Quade. "You say two dozen, Lieutenant?"

"Thereabouts."

"Gentlemen." His face gleaming in the firelight, the Admiral turned to the troops. "Stand or retreat?"

"We'll stand, Admiral," Phillip said. Without a backward glance, but there was no disagreement from Sousa or the other troopers.

A smile eased the hard lines of the Admiral's mouth, softened even more as he looked at Hallie. He gave her a quick squeeze and patted her awkwardly between her shoulder blades.

"Brave girl. I'm proud of you," he said gruffly, then turned her by one arm toward Quade. "Get my granddaughter out of here, Lieutenant. That's an order."

"Aye, sir." Quade held out his hand to her, the flames creeping closer down the hillside flickering in his eyes, on the muscles of his arms, on the barrel of the Uzi.

Hallie took a last look at her grandfather, his face ruddied by the backglow of the fire. This was how she'd remember him, the Admiral in command, straight and tall as a mainmast. She dropped a quick, quivery kiss on his outthrust, Mount Rushmore jaw, caught Quade's hand and ran.

She hoped for her life.

22

THE FIRE CHASED THEM down the beach, the superheated air sucking Hallie's breath. Sparks and ash steamed in the tide crashing onto the shore where the cay narrowed and cut north.

Quade veered them into the surf, ran them through it to soak their clothes, then pulled her up the sand into the palm trees, into a crouch behind two thick trunks grown together.

Over the crackle of close-by flames, Hallie heard the thud of rapidly approaching footsteps. A lot of them. Peering through the crotch of the trees, she saw Mai Lu's two-dozen heavily armed troops, led by the Dragon Lady herself, an Uzi in her hands rather than a parasol. Her drop-dead figure was hidden by fatigues. The fire lit her eyes, glistened in the camouflage paint on her face, the smile on her moist red mouth.

When the column had jogged past, Quade pulled her up and tugged her through the trees toward the house and the dock.

"Isn't this the wrong way?" Hallie asked.

"It's the only way at the moment."

"Why did you light the bonfire?"

"I didn't. Sharkskin did. Then Conan shot him from the deck of the cruiser." He glanced at her, the Uzi slung over his right shoulder and tucked under his arm ready to use. "How d'you think I got this?"

He'd taken Sharkskin's watch, too. The digital face winked the time at her from his wrist—seven-twenty. "But why did he light the fire?"

"I'd say he is—or was—as big a fanatic as Mai Lu."

"Let me guess. Conan shot him because he didn't want *his* fireworks upstaged by yours."

"Gold star on your chart, Rhodes scholar." Quade coughed in the smoke thickening around them, glanced over his shoulder to make sure Mai Lu hadn't left a rear guard, and drew Hallie out of the trees. "With any luck," he said, pulling her into a run, "Mai Lu left her troop carrier on the beach."

She hadn't. A one-way, die-for-the-cause mission, Hallie thought, stumbling into Quade as they rounded a clump of palms jutting across the sand and he yanked her into them. She peeked around his shoulder, saw the cruiser at the dock and Conan on deck. No sign of an Uzi, but that didn't mean he didn't have one.

"Now what?" she whispered.

"I'm thinking."

Lights dipped and flickered in the twilight deepening over the mouth of the bay—the gunboats lying in wait for the *Joanna*. The jungle behind the house was starting to smolder. A burst of automatic fire made Hallie spin around.

"His choice, tough girl."

"I'm not tough," she said, blinking at him through tears.

"I know." Quade smiled. "But I won't tell anybody."

Another high-pitched rat-a-rat-a volley from the Uzis echoed up the beach. The deep thoom-thoom of the AK-47s the Admiral's men carried brought Conan to the rail. With a bullhorn, not an Uzi.

"Mr. Quade, Miss Stockton." His amplified voice was pleasant as always. "I do wish you'd hurry. Our safety margin is diminishing. I can only wait another five minutes."

"Son of a bitch," Quade said, a slow grin spreading across his gleaming, ash-blackened face.

Hallie couldn't believe it. "Can we trust him?"

"Hell no." Quade unlooped the Uzi from his shoulder in a sign of peace. "But I'll kiss his big ugly mug if he'll get us off this time bomb."

Conan saw them—and the Uzi held by its strap in Quade's hand—smiled and spread his palms on the rail as they approached. "At last. I was beginning to worry."

"So was I," Quade replied, lifting one foot onto the dock. "Why the change of heart?"

"I'm a businessman, Mr. Quade. Competition is good for business, and you're the best I've faced in some time. May I offer you a truce? And a lift?"

"Where are you headed?"

"Away from here as fast and as far as possible."

"Then permission to come aboard, Captain," Quade said, lifting Hallie by her elbow onto the dock.

"Granted." Conan offered his big right hand to help her.

A prolonged exchange of gunfire froze Hallie's fingers inches from his and turned her head one last time down the dark strip of beach. Long fingers of orange flame leaped above the jungle. She felt Quade's eyes on her, and Conan's, then lifted her chin and squared her shoulders. She was the granddaughter of an admiral and she wouldn't shame him. She took Conan's hand and stepped aboard.

Hallie didn't understand the choice her grandfather had made, nor was she at all sure he had, but she respected his right to make it. It was more than he'd ever done for her, but at the moment that didn't seem important.

What was important was getting out of here. She coiled and stowed the lines Quade tossed her as he jumped aboard, then followed him and Conan into the wheelhouse. She wanted to but didn't look back at Shark Island when the cruiser pulled away from the dock and swung toward the open water.

"I suggest you stay out of sight until we clear this nest of lunatic extremists," Conan told them from the wheel, his gaze intent on the water, his face ruddied by fire glow.

"If that's your opinion of them," Hallie said, sliding onto a portside bench he indicated beside Quade, "why did you work for Mai Lu?"

"Business, Miss Stockton," he replied with a thin smile, "sometimes makes stranger bedfellows than politics."

Then he picked up the microphone and spoke into the radio. Two of the gunboats prowling the mouth of the bay broke formation to allow the cruiser through. Once it streaked past in a wake turned gold and orange by the blaze and the remnants of the sunset, the gunboats closed ranks.

"Pays to have friends in low places," Quade murmured.

The fire dimmed as the distance between the cruiser and the island lengthened. Every minute or two Conan broadcasted an identification code so no one would shoot them by mistake.

When the charges blew in a terrible, earsplitting roar, Hallie wheeled to her feet, pressed against the bullet-proof plexiglass enclosing the wheelhouse and stared at the orange fireball expanding on the western horizon. It was huge, illuminated the sky and the dark water with a hellish glow and gleamed in the reflection of Quade's face behind her.

"I wish we had boatswain's pipes," Hallie said, the tears in her eyes bleeding into her voice. "I don't understand why he stayed, why Phillip and John and Sousa stayed with him. I don't even understand why I'm crying."

"He had his moments," Quade said. "There was a time when I would've followed him into hell."

"You did." Hallie met his eyes in his reflection. "And look what it got you."

"You really shouldn't watch, Miss Stockton," Conan said. "That bright a glare isn't at all good for your corneas."

"Down, girl." Quade caught her arms when she whipped toward Conan. "This is only a truce."

And this was his world, not hers. The only one she'd ever known, dysfunctional as it was, had just been blown to smithereens by the man at the wheel. The man with no name and no history, who was worried about her corneas.

For money, not for a cause or to avenge a death like Mai Lu. This was business, Quade's business as much as Conan's. Yet she loved him, so much that it hurt to see the dirt and fatigue smearing his face, the singed spot on his left brow.

Hallie felt herself starting to shake, knew it was reaction and shock, but knowing didn't help. She wanted off this boat, away from both of them, out of this nightmare.

"Why aren't *you* watching?" Hallie snapped at Conan. "I should think you'd want to admire your handiwork."

"I'm a bit busy at the moment." He glanced over his shoulder, catching Quade's eye, not hers. "The shock wave from the blast will be along presently."

In the next instant the cruiser began to buck and pitched Hallie against Quade's chest. She flung her arms around him reflexively, he caught the hand bar above the port bench as the cruiser rolled beneath them. The engines roared and whined, sputtered but held.

A massive wave broke over the prow, another crashed over the stern and flooded the deck, washing seawater under the hatch. Hallie slipped and clung to Quade, Conan to the wheel. Big and powerful as the boat was, it tossed like a toy under the faucet in a bathtub. But for seconds only, until the tsunami passed, leaving the cruiser rocking broadside in its wake, with gentler waves slapping the hull.

"That wasn't so bad," Conan observed, turning to nod gallantly at Hallie. "I'd be pleased if you'd take the main cabin, Miss Stockton. You look all-in."

"C'mon." Quade caught her arm. "I'll tuck you in."

Hallie took a quick backward look at the fireball still leaping in the west. Not as high, not as bright. Then she followed Quade down the main hatchway.

"I'd join you," he told her with a tired smile, when they reached the cabin. "But I think I'll keep an eye on our friend tonight."

"I don't understand anything anymore." Hallie leaned numbly against the bulkhead. "Conan did Mai Lu's bidding, yet he put himself at risk to save us. Why?"

"I don't know." Quade wiped his ash-blackened forehead. "Why don't you ask him?"

Hallie did the next morning when she came topside into the dazzling sunlight flooding the wheelhouse. Conan smiled and handed her a mug of coffee.

"I admire your spirit and ingenuity, Miss Stockton, and Mr. Quade's skills. It's as simple as that."

More confused than ever, Hallie went out on deck. There was smoke on the horizon, a slow drift toward the south. She shivered and looked away from it, sat down beside Quade on the port bench where he leaned with his elbows on the rail, and told him what Conan had said.

"Floats my boat," he replied with a shrug.

"Is anything ever that simple?"

Quade lifted his sunglasses and looked at her. Hallie had lost hers and squinted at him in the glare of the sun on the water. "Everything's that simple," he said, then dropped his shades and stretched out again against the rail.

After breakfast Quade plotted a course for Luzon. Conan took the wheel and the cruiser headed north toward Manila. Hallie sat on deck, watching the thin trail of smoke dissipate slowly over the horizon.

At midday they saw the sail. Quade watched it through the cruiser's binoculars for about an hour, then stepped into the wheelhouse. Hallie felt their course change in the shift of the wind tugging her hair, glanced questioningly at Quade when he came back on deck.

"It's *Halimedes*," he said.

"Arnie?" Hallie blinked at him, stunned. "What's he doing *here*? How'd he get here so *fast*?"

"Beats me." Quade looked at her with his mirrored eyes. "Why don't you ask him?"

Hallie's heart pounded with trepidation. Arnie was the only anchor she had, yet he'd probably turn handsprings to hear the Admiral was dead. Hallie didn't blame him. She didn't blame anybody, really. Not even Conan.

Within a quarter hour, the angle and dip of *Halimedes'* sails changed. Arnie had seen them, was correcting his own course to meet them. He would come as close as he could, then drop anchor and let the cruiser come alongside. The wheelhouse hatch opened and shut and Conan stepped onto the deck, stretching and rolling his shoulders.

Neither he nor Quade had slept. They'd stayed awake all night, watching each other. Conan's khaki pants and yellow shirt were creased from the hours he'd spent at the wheel.

"Mr. Quade has consented to handle the docking," he explained with a smile. "He's a far better sailor than I."

Hallie tried to smile back at him but couldn't quite manage it. He didn't seem to mind and came to stand at the rail with her, leaving a comfortable six or so feet between them. *A killer, a paid assassin, but not without sensitivity.*

"Thank you for saving our lives."

"You're welcome, Miss Stockton." He inclined his chin. "It was my pleasure."

That's all they said to each other. Hallie owed him her life and Quade's, yet she hoped to God she'd never set eyes on him again.

That was pretty much what she saw on Arnie's face when the cruiser drew near enough to *Halimedes* to make out his features—utter joy at seeing someone he never thought he'd see again. His gaze flicked anxiously toward Conan, then he made a hasty wipe across his eyes with his sleeve.

Much as Hallie did when the cruiser bumped lightly up against *Halimedes.* Quade cut the engines and Conan threw out the anchor. She caught the rope ladder Arnie tossed over the side, Conan held it steady, and she scrambled up into her father's arms.

Hallie didn't see Maxwell until she'd turned out of Arnie's embrace. He gave her a smile that didn't come anywhere near his eyes. She was still trying to decide if she was going to kick him, punch him or spit in his face when Quade came up the ladder and over the side.

He tossed Conan a wave, then wheeled on Arnie and snapped him a salute. A quick, vicious, ugly salute.

"Permission to knock your goddamn teeth down your goddamn throat, *sir*," Quade said and hit him, hard enough to sprawl him on the deck.

"Arnie!" Hallie dropped to the deck beside her father, but he was already shaking his head and pushing himself up on one hand. She looped an arm around his shoulders, flung a sharp upward glare at Quade. "What's *wrong* with you?"

"You wanna tell your daughter how you *knew* where she was, Commander?" Quade flexed the fingers of his right hand against his left. "You wanna tell her how you got here so *fast*? Or you want me to?"

"There's no need for this, Ellison." Maxwell stepped up behind him and laid a hand on his shoulder. "It's over."

"No, it isn't. Not until somebody tells her."

"It wasn't supposed to happen like this," Arnie said.

Not to her, but to Quade. Hallie felt her heart pound against her ribs, heard the cruiser's engines kick over.

"You can't think," Arnie went on, backhanding a trickle of blood from his mouth, "that I'd do anything to jeopardize my daughter, my only child."

"I don't think you did, I *know* you did. You damn near got her blown to hell with the Admiral."

The back of Arnie's wrist froze against the corner of his mouth. "He's dead?"

"Buried at sea," Quade said. "All over the South China Sea with Mai Lu and Christ knows how many others. Happy?"

"Yes, I am." Arnie tried to stand but couldn't, put his arm around Hallie and let her help him up. "I was a fool to trust Mai Lu, I admit it. I didn't realize she'd reneged on our deal until Conan followed Hallie to L.A."

Hallie felt the muscles in his arm and her own pulse jump when she looked at Quade and saw tundra in his eyes. Maxwell glanced away from her, out to sea to watch the cruiser slip away from *Halimedes*.

"What deal?" Hallie demanded, backing away from Arnie.

"The one I made with Mai Lu to get you out of Middleburg." Arnie looked at her at last, his bottom lip swelling. "I hauled bamboo and—well—other stuff for her for a couple years to buy *Halimedes*. I heard her story around the islands, put two and two together and got four.

"I told her the Admiral was as possessive of you as he had been of Jo, that if you managed to get free of him he'd come after you. She said she'd help me. I had to swear not to tell you. It would've worked, except the Admiral didn't come. He sent Quade instead."

"Conan hatched the plan to get me out of Middleburg?" Hallie asked Arnie. "Not you?"

He nodded. She walked away from him, wrapped her hands around the rail to keep herself from screaming or jumping overboard.

"I'm sorry, Hallie," Arnie said. "I'd tried everything to see you. The Admiral wouldn't budge. Then I found out

I—I hadn't much time left. I got desperate. I grabbed the only straw I had."

"It's okay, Arnie." Hallie bit her bottom lip and blinked back tears.

"I'll be below with an ice bag if you want to talk."

She watched her father go with Maxwell behind him. When the hatch slapped shut, Hallie turned around and looked at Quade. He was still rubbing his right hand.

"I hope you broke your fingers," she said.

"This time I may have," he said, flexing them and wincing.

"Thanks, tough guy. Thanks a lot." Hallie spread her hands on the rail behind her. "I needed to hear this now like I need a hole in my head. The Admiral wasn't much, but for most of my life he was all I had. Now Arnie's all I've got, and not for very damn long. Couldn't you have *waited*? Given me a chance to catch my breath?"

Quade looked up at her from his already-bruising knuckles. "If you want me to apologize, forget it. He's goddamn lucky I didn't break his neck."

"He's *dying!*" Hallie shrieked, tears spilling down her face. "He was desperate. I'm all he has left."

"Sounds like the Admiral, doesn't he?"

Hallie thought about slapping him but didn't. She simply clenched her jaw, turned on her heel and went below to tell her father she still loved him. She wasn't sure about Ellison Quade.

23

THE ONLY PLACE WORSE than a mosquito-infested tropical island was Washington D.C. in January. Bombs and all, Quade would have given his eye teeth to be back on Shark Island just to be with Hallie.

She wasn't in Washington. She wasn't with him. She was with Arnie aboard *Halimedes*, taking her time sailing back to Honolulu "to sort things out." He still couldn't believe she'd used that hackneyed phrase on him. With her IQ, he'd have thought she could come up with something more original.

The *Washington Post* called the Admiral's death a "tragic accident," the *Wall Street Journal*, a "great loss to the nation." He'd been killed in an earthquake, so the news reports said, while on a mapping expedition funded by the navy.

"Sounds like Jacques eff-ing Cousteau," Quade had said when he read that. Then he'd thrown the paper across the room and reached for his umpteenth Scotch and water, no ice, of the day.

Memorial services, according to *Newsweek*, were pending the return of his granddaughter. She'd been traveling with the Admiral, was "slightly injured" and recovering in a Honolulu hospital.

When the CIA called, Quade went with Max to see the director and told his story. Then the Navy Department called. Hell no, he couldn't prove it, Mr. Secretary, *sir*. He'd been drunk for two, or was it three days after that?

He did a job for Max just to have something to do besides drink. Fairly routine, no glitches. He even managed to keep his mind on it most of the time. He came home to his apartment, to the answering machine flashing the maximum number of messages, and fell over his suitcase getting to it. Reba had called three times. The rest were hang-ups.

He didn't call Reba. He played the tape over and over listening for any background noises in the static that might denote an airport, a marina, *anything*. He had it bad. Bad enough for Scotch with no water, and very little lining left in his stomach after that.

The next day, a Friday, his doorbell rang. This time he fell over the couch. His mother stood in the hallway. He was so glad to see her he couldn't speak, yet so disappointed his eyes filled. She didn't know the difference and held her arms out to him with misty eyes of her own.

The next weekend he went home to Bethesda, to the house he'd grown up in and hadn't seen in seven years. The Mustang wasn't what she'd once been, but neither was he. His insurance agent had yet to return his calls.

His father was standing outside waiting for him, a corduroy jacket with leather elbows over his sweater, a muffler around his neck. He took his hands out of his pockets when Quade got out of the car, held out his right one. When his son took it, he threw his left arm around his shoulders.

"If Hiram Whitcomb weren't already dead, I'd kill him," he said, and started to cry.

They were a long time getting into the house. His mother never said a word.

On Monday morning the Navy Department called again. He saw his father's fine hand in that, but went to see the secretary anyway. A week later his father called

to tell him the Admiral's memorial service was sched-
uled for eleven o'clock, two days later, at the National
Cathedral.

His father had read about it in the *Post*. That gave
Quade a jolt and his answer, still he got a haircut, polished his shoes and dressed carefully with a black arm-
band over the sleeve of his gray suede blazer and went to
pay his last respects. Ambivalent though they were.

He saw Hallie in the front pew with Arnie. Her hair
shone like pewter in a shaft of sunlight beaming through
a stained-glass window. Arnie glanced around the
church before the service began, but Hallie stared straight
ahead at the altar and never budged. Quade's throat
ached as he watched her.

The Secretary of the Navy, *sir*, gave the eulogy, the
chaplin who'd served last aboard ship with the Admiral
prayed for his immortal soul. All the top brass were there.
One or two nodded to him.

He waited outside after the service, close enough to the
family limousine to make sure Hallie saw him. She did,
once Arnie wrenched her out of the pack of reporters. In
a sleek black suit and fur piece, she froze as the chauf-
feur opened the rear door, one dark-stockinged leg lifted.
Quade started toward her, but her lashes swept down
and she ducked inside the car.

He thought about chasing her, throwing himself on the
rear deck the way Conan had, pounding on the window
and shouting at her to stop, stop. He was a prince again,
the enchantment had been lifted. But he didn't. He
walked back to the Mustang and drove to Bethesda.

His mother was thrilled to see him, delighted that he'd
just dropped in like he'd used to. His father stirred out of
a nap with the newspaper and a smile. They took the
dogs for a walk and he stayed for supper.

Macaroni and cheese made from scratch, peas and applesauce, his mother's meat loaf made with Ritz crackers and tomato soup. It fell apart on your fork but, God, was it good. He let himself cry on I-90, whizzing along at sixty-five with the back end of the Mustang shimmying. This wasn't how fairy tales were supposed to end, goddammit. They were supposed to end happily.

He was out of Scotch, thought about stopping to buy a bottle, but didn't. He got off the elevator at nine-seventeen, saw Hallie sitting on the floor next to his door and stopped.

He couldn't believe it, even when she did a slow slide up the wall, pushing herself upright in her two-inch, blue suede over-the-knee boots. She wore the blue suede dress and her silver fox. Quade wanted to kiss her knees.

Hallie wanted to wrap herself around him and bury her face in his chest the way she had in San Francisco. Wanted to so badly she could almost smell his suede jacket and cigarettes across the twelve feet of carpeted hallway that separated them.

But she wasn't sure he wanted her to, wasn't sure the dress and the boots were such a hot idea after all. She wasn't sure of anything except she loved him, that if he didn't move or say something in the next ten seconds she was going to splinter into little pieces.

"Hey, tough girl," he said, walking slowly toward her.

The singed spot was still in his left eyebrow. The burn had faded but the bald spot would be there for a while.

"Hey, tough guy." Hallie smiled, felt her lips tremble and hoped she didn't look like she was about to cry. Even though she was.

"Cup of coffee?" he asked, stopping next to her to unlock his door. Hardly brilliant, only slightly better than "Coffee, tea or me?" but it was an opening.

"Yes, thank you."

Quade opened the door and moved aside, drew a deep breath as she stepped past him and inhaled Chanel No. 5. His mouth watered. He followed her inside, shut the door and held her jacket. She slid out of it, moved across the living room looking around, turned to face him on the other side of the gray sectional.

She wore her mother's pearls. They caught the light of the porcelain ginger-jar lamp he'd left on and gleamed in the hollow of her throat. Quade's heart started to pound.

"It was nice of you to come today," Hallie said, resisting the urge to fling herself at him. "Thank you."

"I didn't come for the Admiral." He tossed the silver fox over the back of the couch and looked at her, his eyes dark and smoky. "I came for you."

"I wanted to talk to you, but not in the middle of a media circus."

And not with the Admiral still hovering between them. She wanted to tell him that, tell him the hardest thing she'd ever done was get in that limo, but she couldn't.

"You got off pretty lucky," he said with a shrug. "Arnie did a good job of crowd control."

"You were right about him," Hallie said. "He's almost as possessive as the Admiral."

Arnie hadn't wanted her to come, was still sore at Quade for slugging him.

"But we make allowances, don't we? After all, he's dying."

There was no malice in his voice. Hurt maybe, but Hallie wasn't sure. There was something different about him, something changed, but she couldn't decide what.

"Maybe not quite so soon," she told him. "I dragged him kicking and screaming to Bethesda. He's in remission."

"I'm glad," Quade said, and meant it.

He didn't want to strangle Arnie anymore. He just wanted to spend the rest of his life with his daughter.

"I came to tell you that, and tell you I'm not pregnant." Hallie dropped her gaze, her voice shaking, caught a knotted piece of fringe between her fingers and twisted it. "I also came to tell you I wouldn't mind getting that way."

Quade felt his throat swell as she lifted her eyes, her beautiful amber-brown eyes and said haltingly, "If you still want me."

Did he ever. He wanted to leap over the couch and take her right there and then on the floor. Instead he took off his blazer and laid it over her silver fox.

"There's something you ought to see first," he said, heading toward the bedroom. "Wait here."

Hallie did, chilled to the bone. She twisted her fringe, twisted her fingers together and paced a small, tight circle looking around and wishing he'd come back.

It only took Quade three minutes to change. When he came back into the living room Hallie was flipping through his Elvis albums in the oak cabinet by the stereo. She turned when he cleared his throat, her breath catching visibly. Her face, he thought, shone brighter than the brass buttons he'd spent all of yesterday afternoon polishing.

"Oh, *Ellison*." She breathed his name with the extra l's he loved, her eyes glistening. "I mean." She snapped

to attention and clicked her heels. No Annapolis grad
had ever done it better. "Lieutenant Quade."

"Captain in a year if I keep my nose clean. What d'you
think?" He glanced down and tugged at the hem of his
uniform jacket. "Is it me?"

He lifted his head and looked at her, a lock of hair falling over his forehead. Hallie already knew he looked
good in white, but she'd had no idea anybody could look
so breathtaking in navy blue and gold braid.

"You bet." She nodded, still at attention.

Quade drew a deep breath. "Is it you?"

"Oh, *yes*." Hallie felt her chin quaver but held her salute.

"At ease, sailor."

At last he returned the salute, then stepped forward to
catch her when she ran into his arms, laughing around
the bubble of tears in her voice. "I love you." She clung
to him, trembling. "I was an idiot and I'm sorry, but I love
you."

"You weren't an idiot. *I* was an idiot." Quade caught
her hair in his left hand and tugged her head back. "I
don't report for six weeks. That's time for a wedding and
a honeymoon, isn't it?"

"*We* don't report for six weeks," Hallie corrected him.
"Where to?"

"Pensacola on March first." Quade looped his right
arm around her waist. "Tomorrow in Bethesda to tell
Mom and Dad."

Not Admiral and Mrs. Ellison Quade II. That's what
was different, that's what had changed. Hallie bit her lip
and blinked back tears.

"Don't worry, they'll love you." Quade pulled her
close and gave her a hey-baby smile. "So do I, by the way.

With every hot, horny little inch of me, I love you, Hallie Stockton Quade."

Hallie bumped her forehead against his chin to hide her tears. "Bit premature, aren't you?"

"Set a date fast." He tightened his hand on her hair, tipped her head back and grinned. "Or Ellison H. Quade IV will be."

"What's the *H* for?"

"You'll find out when we fill in the birth certificate." Quade caught her hand, tried to lead her into the bedroom but she dug in her heels. Those magnificent two-inch, blue suede heels.

"Ellison," she said, giving a sharp edge to the *l*.

"Horatio."

"Not my kid."

"*Our* kid."

"Not *our* kid."

"It's tradition."

Hallie thought about it for all of two seconds, then shrugged and said, "Okay."

Quade led her into the bedroom, unzipped her dress and stepped her out of it. "I want you to do one more thing for me," he murmured against her mouth as he lowered her onto the bed.

"For you, tough guy, anything." Hallie wound her arms around his neck and sighed. "What is it?"

"Leave your boots on."

A Note from Lynn Michaels

Like the best emeralds, the most interesting heroes have flaws. It's their imperfections that make them alluring—for the writer as well as the reader. These "defects" catch your eye and your breath, add depth and dimension to the story.

When I first envisioned *The Patriot*, I thought Nevin Maxwell was the hero. But when the phone rang at the beginning of chapter one, Ellison Quade answered. He talked and I listened. He told me about himself, about the Admiral and Max, but mostly he told me about Hallie. "Just get me on a plane for L.A.," he said. "I'll take care of the rest."

Which he did. Up to a point. The most important part of the story he left to Hallie. Making Quade lovable wasn't a problem—what woman in her right mind wouldn't fall for a sexy gray-eyed Scorpio, with hidden, unplumbed depths—the challenge was making him believe he was lovable. Flaws and all. It took her a while, but Hallie convinced him. Admirably.

And irrevocably.

Books by Lynn Michaels

HARLEQUIN TEMPTATION
304–REMEMBRANCE

Rebels & Rogues

Dash vowed to protect gorgeous
Claren—at any cost!

The Knight in Shining Armor
by JoAnn Ross
Temptation #409, September

All men are not created equal. Some are rough
around the edges. Tough-minded but
tenderhearted. Incredibly sexy. The tempting
fulfillment of every woman's fantasy.

When it's time to fight for what they believe in, to
win that special woman, our Rebels and Rogues are
heroes at heart. Twelve Rebels and Rogues, one
each month in 1992, only from Harlequin
Temptation. Don't miss the upcoming books by
our fabulous authors, including Ruth Jean Dale,
Janice Kaiser and Kelly Street.

JAYNE ANN KRENTZ

A two-part epic tale from one of today's most popular romance novelists!

Dreams
Parts One & Two

The warrior died at her feet, his blood running out of the cave entrance and mingling with the waterfall. With his last breath he cursed the woman— told her that her spirit would remain chained in the cave forever until a child was created and born there....

So goes the ancient legend of the Chained Lady and the curse that bound her throughout the ages—until destiny brought Diana Prentice and Colby Savager together under the influence of forces beyond their understanding. Suddenly they were both haunted by dreams that linked past and present, while their waking hours were filled with danger. Only when Colby, Diana's modern-day warrior, learned to love, could those dark forces be vanquished. Only then could Diana set the Chained Lady free....

Available in September wherever Harlequin books are sold.

JK92